AF572427

# losing michael malone

# losing michael malone

Nicholas Kasunic

Tate Publishing & *Enterprises*

*Losing Michael Malone*
Copyright © 2010 by Nicholas Kasunic. All rights reserved.

No part of this publication may be reproduced, stored in a retrieval system or transmitted in any way by any means, electronic, mechanical, photocopy, recording or otherwise without the prior permission of the author except as provided by USA copyright law.

**This novel is a work of fiction. Names, descriptions, entities, and incidents included in the story are products of the author's imagination. Any resemblance to actual persons, events, and entities is entirely coincidental.**

The opinions expressed by the author are not necessarily those of Tate Publishing, LLC.

Published by Tate Publishing & Enterprises, LLC
127 E. Trade Center Terrace | Mustang, Oklahoma 73064 USA
1.888.361.9473 | www.tatepublishing.com

Tate Publishing is committed to excellence in the publishing industry. The company reflects the philosophy established by the founders, based on Psalm 68:11,
*"The Lord gave the word and great was the company of those who published it."*

Book design copyright © 2010 by Tate Publishing, LLC. All rights reserved.
*Cover design by Kellie Southerland*
*Interior design by Nathan Harmony*

Published in the United States of America

ISBN: 978-1-61739-375-4
1. Fiction: General
2. Fiction: Coming of Age
10.11.29

# acknowledgements

I am obliged to acknowledge the miserable pain of life, and am privileged to experience a beautiful life of pain.

The readers, editors, and support that made this work possible:

This work's editor, Aubrey.

Mary Claire, Jon, Julia, Susan, Sean, Beth, Eek, Maddie, Raquel, Elise, Anna, Ed, Hay, Justin, Amanda, Phil, Beth, Adrienne, Gerry, the Authonomy Community, Mollie, Dawn, Zeke, Julia, Rachel, Danika, Patty, Bob, Jake, Brandon, Mayanna, Lisa and all of those not mentioned but who undoubtedly helped.

*pain [ˈpān]*

*–noun*

*1.*

*physical suffering or distress, as due to injury, illness, etc.*

*2.*

*a distressing sensation in a particular part of the body: a back pain.*

*3.*

*mental or emotional suffering or torment: I am sorry my news causes you such pain.*

*bliss [blis]*

*–noun*

*1.*

*supreme happiness; utter joy or contentment*

*2.*

*The joy of heaven*

*3.*

*heaven; paradise*

This is a collection of neither, or both.

# preface

The viewing was today—a day, in description, no different than the next. Those that solemnly arrived brought gloom to the clouds and acidity to the rain. Everything along the pathway to the side doors of the funeral parlor was too far to touch, too bland to understand. The luscious grass and intricately arranged flowerbeds were too vibrant for the moment and evoked a detached sensation of how things might have been before death arrived. The small, feathery, Japanese maple situated next to the entrance became a blurred haze of green each time the crossing wind combed through the sapling's branches and cascaded each rippling leaf over the next. The half-cylindrical awnings over the stairs created a claustrophobic tunnel, and the nine, air-tight, cement steps resonated with shouts of harrowing warning through the heel, into the buckling knee, as life moved forward to face the reality of Death.

Inside the parlor, a girl no older than twenty slowly waded through the crowd. She was a spectator—no one appeared to know her, except perhaps the deceased. The air was so thick that the blackness of everyone's attire became a collective shadow, choking all light. An aura of cologne and perfume hovered around each individual in a smoky fear, like a fragile repellent against the stale odor of death—one of mothballs and pine-scented disinfectant.

*Few people knew what actual death smelled like*, thought the girl, as she sniffed and smiled at the redolence of two, assuring tells of good housekeeping. The true stench of death seeps into every pore and breathes into every orifice of the privileged audience to human expiration. Thus, the living that are present have no choice but to inhale death into their lungs and let it course through their veins, despite feeling as if their own blood had lost all rhythm and understanding to its fundamental purpose. They become terrified to the point of stoicism, and stare into the eyes of a corpse that can no longer look back, only through.

The girl slowly breathed in through her nose, still captivated by her thought. If the livings in attendance act accordingly, they will be forever marked by the deception of those vacant eyes, the unequivocal emptiness of death, and the smell that it leaves as a legacy.

The girl breathed out, and her shoulders dropped. She supposed, however, if mothballs and cleaner fluid hinted at similar symptoms, she too would consider breaking the bank for a few ounces of Clive Christian's finest.

It was easier for her, than anyone else, to move about the room. Most everyone surrendered to obligation, held prisoner, shifting weight from one foot to the other while uttering sighs of intentional sorrow poisoned by unavoidable, yet regretful boredom.

The girl sat down in an empty armchair in an adjacent hallway, and pulled out a thin, blue notebook from her purse. She opened to the first page dated over four years ago.

*January 6, 2004*

*I am not ready to die, but I no longer wish to continue this life.*

She rolled her eyes at the failed philosophy of the entry, but not without a twinge of disdain for her private disrespect. The self-consciousness of her presence heightened, and she quickly closed and stored the booklet before someone asked where she got it from. Tossing it in her purse reminded her that she kept it only out of obligation, for her interaction with the journal caused more spite than she ever intended.

The girl looked into the stagnant mess of people who had come to pay their respects to a young man whom most of them barely knew.

Her stare fell onto the journal that peeked out of the darkness of her purse, but just as quickly returned to the main room, where a small number of persons particularly stood out beyond the generic standards of mourning. Though their dress and demeanor alike were appropriately similar to the rest, the girl could not help but take note of the acute suffering she felt in them as she looked at each subject.

The mother of the deceased was easy to locate, for a long line of visitors patiently waited to hold her outstretched hand and say "sorry," not only for her loss or for the futility of her son's fight, but because there was nothing else to say.

The girl watched as the mother graciously appreciated every offer of condolences and accepted every tear shed at her feet. Her strength was ironically painful, thought the girl; this woman was too practiced in hurt.

The outsider's observation traveled beyond the mother, to a heaving figure that could only embody the boy's father. He did not need to shun anyone away—people either understood the necessary boundaries of his grief, or feared the contagious misery of his presence.

He shoved his face into the palms of his hands, and raked his fingers down his forehead. He wanted the room to feel his pain, out of loyalty to his son. Unnecessary, the girl thought.

A young, stern-looking woman walked briskly to his side, and lightly touched the tips of the father's fingers.

He rose instantly and hugged the woman, relieving more of his weight than he probably should have.

The woman anchored her legs against the load, and propped her chin atop his slouching shoulder, her face fully visible to anyone witnessing the embrace. She showed no signs of emotion—only frantic thought that tightened the skin across her cheeks.

As the woman gingerly guided the father back onto the couch and exited in a determined stride elsewhere, the girl, still sitting idly in the hallway, leaned back into the armchair hoping that the woman wouldn't catch her line of sight. She averted her eyes from this emotionally ambiguous female, still unsure if the woman was a close family member, or the funeral director. Confused, she turned her head, returning to the personality that originally caught her eye.

A small, frail young woman who was softly pigmented by an unblemished white stood silently in a corner. Her right arm hung firmly to her side, and held a half-filled bottle of water. Her left arm loosely clung to her right's bicep, while her head and shoulders pointed shyly toward the ground. There was something brilliant about her, as her presence was illuminated by something completely opposite to a spotlight. Her gaze slowly lifted with a severity so trained that it must have been applied to everything she did.

The anonymous viewpoint in the hallway, now holding the blue journal with both hands, could not help but follow this woman's eyes to the most conspicuous body in the room.

A stiffness mounted the girl's spine, and she packed away the wrinkled journal of Michael Malone, a dead man.

There is not necessarily a story to these people. Moreover, there is a feeling to them, a much needed provocation of sensibility.

Their end, however, is quite noteworthy, as we all have, at the very least, a life that precedes an end, and an end worth printing.

*Michael Malone*

*Age 19, of Brooklyn, on Thursday, April 3, 2008. Cherished son of Jack and Kathryn Malone. He will be survived by the entirety of the loving Malone family, and all those who crossed paths with his strength, joy, and love. Friends will be received Friday, April 4, 2–4 and 6–8pm in the Peter J. Lawrence Funeral Home. Funeral service will be held Saturday at 11:30am in Our Lady of Grace Church. Interment will be in the All Souls Cemetery.*

# part 1

## *passion*

Each snowflake melted at the moment of its landing on the outside of the window, which was thoroughly heated by the tiring radiator below it. Across the room, the other window was defiantly propped open to welcome the cool, yet refreshing thirty-two degree wind that herded numerous fleeing, dead leaves begging for a final resting place. A steady whirring of a groundskeeper's loyal talk-radio competed with the uninterrupted melody of car engines coughing awake in the parking lot, while the wind, in jealousy, made its own, determined efforts for attention by washing over the leaves of the trees and coolly whistling down the thinnest of alley ways.

The buzzing hum of flirtatious whispers from the two lovers next door were drowned out by the wailing dissonance of an alarm that seemed to bother everyone in the apartment complex but the *free spirits* (with robotic tendencies) bedside to it. They were too busy to do anything but have sex and then complement their screams of elation with Alzheimer-like conversation, routine cooperation with the classic one-fork-for-two coupled eating, and an unfailing tuck of the hair behind the ear or an affectionate struggle for the last bite of cake (repeat steps 1–3).

The sun was steadfastly peering through the threatening clouds, proud to be a reason for all of the beautiful landscape that graced the hilly backdrop of a bustling and vivacious city. Birds produced the lively but deliberate soundtrack, and the citizens heading to work, coffee in hand, individually whistled a personal tune—as if they absolutely knew that their instrumental accompaniment added to the grand opening of a long-time standing, highly regarded show. Emma, still in bed, lifted her eyelids and sighed with a bitter wisdom of the persevering monotony of intrusive sunlight, false cheer, and inevitable, soul-sedating interaction that awaited her.

She wasn't shy; she simply didn't appreciate the *art* of conversation, as her father had always advertised it to his incredibly talented but purposefully inarticulate daughter. As she put it—this *art*, unlike her paintings and writings, was an incessant and unnecessary recitation of previous practice in boring a fellow stranger during coercion of social awkwardness. However, she devotedly condemned the use of *her* art as well. And so this conflicted, inward judgment expanded Emma's exhaustion, repeatedly scraping away at the desperate principles of her barren, but determined existence, like a tortured groove of vinyl endlessly scratched by a skipping needle, until the point of forgotten song.

Academia had been suspiciously easy to her all the way through a college graduation of awards, but this supposed proof of useful prowess she exhibited was no solace. If anything, it instigated further confusion, and a misguided passion impatiently commanded futile action toward anything but fulfillment. Emma was undefined.

She was never a lover despite her emotional allegiance to her mother, and she could not be called a fighter even though more often than not her voice was raised and her words cut deep. Anything in-between would still not be a proper description. Every emotion was there, but the things that prompted her sadness, despair, anger, and frustration seemed trivial to the rest of the world.

She had given up on happiness, or happiness had given up on her. The only consolation was that Emma could be bitterly grateful to feel an absence of something she hardly knew.

She had, however, dissected the notion of love enough to know that her family loved her. So, there was that.

Emma stood in front of the mirror, seeing her pale skin and stolid features in as many shades of grey as she could imagine, so as to ward off any color that might plague her disillusioned eyes—there was no color that could fill her doleful manner. Though she was fully aware of the general happiness that would swarm around her without fail as she backed out of the main lobby door carrying briefcases dripping with loose, overcrowded papers, she was self-assuredly unable to ignorantly sing along with choir. It's not that she was tone-deaf; she just didn't understand what she was singing for—there was no true, elegant finale in sight, just abrupt endings when the director signaled the end of a piece mid-note. What was everyone so happy about? Was the coffee that good? Even if it *was* discovered to be the unanimous key to human happiness, Emma wouldn't dare allow her lips to touch the brim of a mug that contained a fresh batch of "life's answer" brewed just this morning—everyone else was doing it.

Emma had always been like this. Not because it distinguished her from the masses (she didn't like crowds anyway), nor did it promote her confidence in the beauty of the individual. It was that she outright, definitively despised most of what the rest of the world was doing. The problem was, embarrassingly, she had no plan or path to take the misled to the land of milk and honey with her.

The tears that had escorted Emma to sleep last night still lingered in the corners of her eyes, like residue left over from a failed experiment. She quickly ran a forearm across her face in a sweeping attempt to forget the daily despair that led to these wretched sobs of uncertainty, most likely returning to her tonight. She turned before the mirror could capture a last look, and loaded a variety of backpacks, briefcases, and satchels onto her bony arms and frail shoulders. It was time to go to work.

As she closed her door to her apartment, a cackling giggle raced under the adjacent door and screeched into her ears—another side effect of lovesickness, a disease that had bed ridden her neighbors for the entire three months of their rent; an infirmity Emma was apparently immune to. Mid-cringe, she wished they would shut up already and get back to the sex. She hated their unintelligent questions and dimwitted responses even more than their over-exaggerated groans. She turned her key and clicked her door shut. Did they ever leave, or did they just bathe in the obvious devotion each had for the other?

Work kept her mindful, but thoughtlessly busy—she liked that. There was not time for the threadless sowing of her negative thoughts.

At lunchtime, Emma left the office and traveled a few miles down the road to the Chinese restaurant on the corner. She stepped into something that resembled a large closet, much bigger than her cubicle at the bank. It contained fifteen or so fidgety students, eager to learn and captivated by their only known professional source of knowledge—Emma. Their greeting to her was that of a loyal brigade to their five-star general the night before a surrender was signed, and they were on the winning side:

"Good afternoon, Ms. Emma!"... It was the way they said it. After all, in order to express their true gratification for her kindness and devoted teaching, it would have to be said in Chinese.

Emma looked back at the shrunken classroom full of late-twenties to mid-thirties Chinese restaurant employees, then to her chair, which pinned a mop and broom to the back wall, and in its seat, cradled a Twinkie and Statue of Liberty—a regular set of gifts from her students. The restaurant manager, who acquired Emma's services via the classifieds, said that, "a knowing of the English," would help improve customer service—even though the business operated in the vast boundaries of Chinatown.

If she hadn't been told, Emma would have had no idea of the twelve-hour days for which each employee nearly volunteered at the restaurant. They all slept, ate and worked around the clock with their family; they all laughed, cried, joked, supported one another—in their family. They experienced what Emma could only pretend to feel.

Emma was an accountant, but one could not accurately number the amount of worthy stories she had to tell. Odd jobs such as this were substantial fodder. " Hey everybody. Aw, thank you so much for these," pointing to what basically represented America to her students. "You really shouldn't get me something every day. But really, thank you." She tried to match their sincerity, but that was impossible.

*Pain is not easily defined. Pain is not hurt, nor is it injury. It is a living, breathing sickness that attacks every part of our lives. We do not see it, but we diagnose it. We cannot bear it, but rarely live without it. Its relativity divides us, and its consequences unite us. We all live pain.*

Heading back to her apartment at around five, she was already becoming stressed. She had invited her parents over for dinner even though she had just been to their house for the same event two nights before. They won't appreciate it. She toppled off the bus, completely unaware that the driver was making disgruntled admonishments to her delayed walk down the aisle, due to the slipping, cumbersome packs that had somehow grown in size since this morning.

She began her dismount once the bus had come to a full stop—"It's not a catwalk missy!" If she had heard it, she would not have been able to realize what she had done wrong. No matter, her brow was furrowed as she continued her prowl toward her apartment. Watching her, one would guess she was suffering from having waited too long to go to the bathroom.

She just had to get dinner ready, but her entrance into her apartment was accompanied by an unavoidable lapse of memory and forgotten agenda. Emma slipped onto the sofa.

Some amount of time later (an exact number of minutes that passed was impossible to recall), there was a knock on the door, reinstalling Emma's surge of intensity. She had forgotten. How had she forgotten? She quickly closed her computer, turned on the stove, and haphazardly threw down a variety of ingredients. Her parents had arrived fifteen minutes early. She obligingly opened the door for them without a word and went back to the kitchen. Her dad watched TV, while her mom loudly voiced family updates from the living room, knowing not to disturb Emma's process.

"Michael said he's sorry he couldn't make it. He won't tear himself away from that journal of his, and actually, I think it's helping—always whipping it out all of a sudden at the dinner table and jotting a thing or two down. He's eating more too." She paused. "I just wish he would've picked it up before."

Emma's father immediately became enamored with the looping infomercial, playing for the second time in two minutes. Emma silently recalled the fact of her brother's actions two months after his prognosis, but didn't want to watch her mother relive the called upon memory. She looked down at her poorly tied shoelaces and allowed time for her Mother's cheek muscles to twitch, eyes to gloss over the growing blackness of their widening pupils, and lower lip to refuse quivering.

Moments like this always made Emma feel uncomfortable. She finally looked up as she heard her mother resume her speech with a wavering attempt at closure—closure that eluded her since Michael's incident over three years ago.

"He's really been quite independent since you graduated from university." There was a distinct aftertaste of guilt in the air, coming from the back of the speaker's throat.

The mother regained any outward composure she might have forgotten. "Your sister seems to be doing a lot better too."

Emma spit out a, "Good. Good," and ducked back into her spice cabinet. After three years, she still didn't know where the paprika was.

Her mother snuck to the edge of the kitchen doorway. The water for the pasta boiled, and so did Emma. Nothing was ready to eat. Her mother poked her head past the borderline, "You want me to do anything, Hon?" She nearly winced.

Emma knew her mom wasn't imposing on or rushing her, and that she really just wanted to spend some time with her daughter. Emma felt safe within her mother's insight and stability; with her mom, her instincts felt comfortable, and not conflicted or contrived or vain. But sometimes what she needed was a black hole for her intrinsic turmoil with the rest of the world. Sometimes she just let everything go.

"Just leave!" Emma blurted. The water was now bubbling over the brim of the pot onto the witch-like fingers of the gas flame. Emma continued, "I didn't even want to have this stupid dinner! Just leave!"

"Emma… Em… Look… " Her mother had bypassed the argument and went straight to the counseling. She partly understood her daughter's misplaced affection. Anyone could laugh with a stranger. Crying meant something.

"No, Mom! Just—leave! I just got back from work, I'm tired, and I just want to eat food that doesn't take forty minutes to make!" All of this was a lie. It was now 7:30, and Emma had somehow forgotten her original panic and absentmindedly watched music videos online for the previous hour. She wasn't tired at all, and food that wasn't personally prepared by herself disgusted her. Her mother knew all this, but did not argue. She had done that for nearly twenty years and nothing had come of it. She pushed her husband toward the door. He was flustered—ordering both women to stop yelling. Neither Emma nor her mom heard him.

"Guess you're making dinner after all," Emma's dad rubbed his wife's back and laughed as he headed to the apartment door. "Love you, honey." He nodded at his daughter.

Emma's mother jerked away from her husband's sarcasm in disgust, approached Emma gently, and kissed her on the forehead. "I'll talk to you soon, Em. I'm sorry."

Emma was still in the kitchen, her fists clenched and knuckles white from a rage that scraped up her skin and boiled any signs of moisture in its victim's eyes. She felt completely helpless. The young woman turned off the stove, feeling a foreign pit of guilt in her stomach, as she pitied the charred and tainted stainless steel. The pot held nothing more than a few droplets of unevaporated water at this point, and Emma so desperately wanted to lick up and relish those surviving tears of fresh water. But what kept her from meeting the throbbing, metal bottom of the pot with her naked tongue was not a fear of pain from burn, nor wariness of scarred taste buds imprisoned to blandness, for she rarely maintained a relationship with the severity of pain, and had grown quite accustomed to the tastelessness of her food.

She didn't eat that night. Later, she texted her mom to apologize. It was nine, and Emma was already falling asleep. She didn't get her mom's two-page text, more easily summarized as a how-to "beat depression" handbook.

The next morning, the leaves had finally managed a way to move into shelter as they hesitantly settled on top of Emma's comforter. She rolled over and denied them access beneath its warmth and security. Minutes later, everything shivered awake to a harsh wind from the open window. Emma opened the fridge—cottage cheese it was for breakfast. Opening the door to leave, the wind passed through, raking through the leaves without mercy.

Heading toward the main lobby, Emma noticed a message monopolizing her cell phone's screen—not allowing her to do anything else on the phone until it was acknowledged. She read it, responded, "Thanks, Mom," and deleted it. Accusations of depression provoked even more despair for her situation. What was her situation? Whatever it was, it was late. If anything, Emma agreed to herself to keep her schedule. Today's first assignment was to make her weekly stop at the branch location and balance their company expense accounts.

She did not realize where she was until she stepped into the lobby of the office building. She tried to recall her commute, but she could not remember a thing between this morning's departure and arrival. The fog of her memory implied as if time had been taken from Emma, subtracting the monotony from her life. It was a wretched feeling.

The elevator lifted to the selected floor, and Emma stepped out. She weaved through the office with her head down, and reached an empty cubicle to gather and organize her various papers. Nearby, two women stood by a water cooler.

"I love your hair like that," a young woman recited her professional courtesy perfectly.

Her company appropriately reciprocated, "Please, I'd die for your volume," and upped the ante, "Plus dying might encourage me to lose a couple pounds."

They were both good and warmed up now. "No! You look great. That pantsuit is so professional. Do you think three unbuttoned is too much for a teller?"

"No, no, no. Keep it. Maybe you'll be lucky enough to find a husband here. This is a bank, you know."

Self-satisfying laughs all around for a well-played surrogacy of assisted vanity.

A slow rumble of sentence fragments interrupted Emma's intently focused hatred for the two women. The mumblings in the cubicle next to Emma sounded so familiar, harnessing her current distaste for humanity. She looked to the water cooler—still a fit of laughs coming from the women that entertained the idea of finding a suitable man in a bank . It was a deeper tone—someone reading her thoughts, someone quietly voicing her opinion about… everything. Emma stood. It was a young man with a distinguished look—the kind of teacher that every girl from her high school class would love to get in bed with. He must have read her diary. No, Emma shook her thoughts. She didn't have a diary.

"Sorry." The same mumbling voice.

At this point Emma had been staring above the man's head for over ten seconds.

“Sorry.” Was she confirming his apology or making her own? She sat down, locking her head straightforward.

The handsome man seesawed his way above the divider between them. Emma could see his swimming, brown eyes and the blanketing, handsome stubble that surrounded his high cheekbones and surprisingly supple lips even from the corner of her eye. He was looking at her and saying something, but Emma, remaining faced forward, was currently deaf by default and waist-deep in a new stack of papers.

The young man sat down, tracing his trained, gelled hair from temple to earlobe. Emma cautiously shot a glance at the cubicle that protected her silence. Conversation avoided.

The next few days Emma continued with her moonlight teaching. Staging a scene between two friends at a restaurant, in English, was just as hard as it looked:

“Hello… *waiter*… could I *have*… a Coke… to *drink*… and just a *salad* with ranch dressing… to start my… *dinner*.” Emma spoke slowly and highlighted each vocabulary word they had been reviewing for the past two weeks. Turning to Bingwen, her handpicked example for the class, “I love this *restaurant*–don’t you?

“Yes. Would you like some fruit?” Bingwen’s voice got surprisingly higher pitched after each word.

“Umm sure. Thanks, Bingwen.” Emma said with a smile. It was from the last lesson, but an articulate and slightly relevant phrase nonetheless. She compromised with a question that she knew would guarantee an answer. "Where are you from?" Emma nearly giggled without a single soul present to identify with her situation.

"Singapore. I love it there." Bingwen beamed to the entire class. They clapped thunderously.

"Okay, everyone. How 'bout we break into groups and talk for a little bit." Emma spoke, but only confirmed her direction with the most body gestures a teacher had ever used.

She smiled to each one of her students as they humbly passed in front of her. She was oddly satisfied by all of their smiling faces. She would tell her brother about this amusing encounter with teaching, and the brief warmth that it brought.

By Friday, Emma knew she had little time left to prepare for the loneliness that waited to spend the weekend with her. Her brother always seemed occupied enough to be unable to answer her open-ended texts. She always missed her mom, but she knew arriving at her parents' doorstep would only instigate concerned, motherly wisdom, and ignorant, fatherly criticism. Anyone Emma was remotely acquainted with was long gone from the city limits, and even if they weren't, they might as well be. Now, angrily saddened, Emma grabbed her car keys and slammed her apartment door shut behind her.

She got as far as the apartment lobby. She couldn't do it. She couldn't bring herself to seek the help she so desperately wanted. She knew her brother was laughing somewhere. She knew her parents were getting comfortable to a movie, and she knew she couldn't be a part of it. She wasn't capable of the happiness everyone else flaunted so casually. All the same, she wished she could go and engage her carefree brother, and bring candy to the private movie showing. She couldn't. Not everyone was so lucky. Her face went blank, erased of any outward sign of total dejection. She drifted back to her cage and locked the barred gate behind her. She found her way to the couch, which she occupied until the next morning.

Saturday was only a confirmation of Friday's haunting. Emma was robbed of any energy she could summon during her draining week of frivolous number crunching. The TV blinked and droned its plethora of primitive sitcoms until Emma squandered her strength to find the remote under the rock of a cushion, and changed the channel. Her brother's favorite show, *It's Always Sunny in Philadelphia* was on:

*Dennis (interrupting his friends' attempts at removing a cat that was stuck in their apartment wall): You guys! I swallowed apple seeds!*

*Dee: So, what?*

*Dennis: Are they poisonous?!*

*Charlie: Are you kidding me, dude? They're extremely poisonous.*

*Dee: They're absolutely not poisonous!*

*Dennis (amidst doubting groans from Charlie): Should I make myself throw up?*

*Charlie: I would throw up—now!*

*Dennis (exiting): Oh, god… d—it!*

*Charlie: Apple seeds, man. That's no good.*

*Dee: Are you kidding me?*

*Charlie: Apple seeds?*

Emma chuckled, but quickly dove back into her sea of thoughts and emotions. She tried to go back to sleep in her purposely darkened apartment—she didn't want to face another empty day full of hopeless activity. Five minutes later, she fought to keep her eyes above half-closed. She hated herself for wasting so much time with unnecessary and unused rest. She swayed from hopelessness to self-loathing, in total frustration, for much of the day. By eight, she was still in her pajamas. Emma showered in her tears, and went back to sleep, still seated upright, contorted to fit her miniature sofa. It was enough defiance directed to her bed to keep her anger at bay. The sun would irritate her in the morning so that she could attend Mass.

Emma sat in the middle of a pew at her local parish. She didn't pray. She participated with the rest of the congregation and executed her public devotion. She had grown too accustomed to a morning, Sunday liturgy to let go of an easy schedule. It was an hour of distraction. God wasn't there for her, and she never expected or even wanted this "Almighty Savior" to be an answer. No one was there for her. She joined in the final blessing, and jolted her mom out of deep prayer to lead their exit from the church.

Weeks had passed and it was Tuesday again. Emma tumbled her way into her weekly cubicle, educating a guess as to which briefcase she should open first.

"Hi," the mumbling voice again.

Emma swiveled around in her chair. She dearly missed his verbal confirmation of her woes with the rest of humanity. "Hello. Good. How are you?" The preemptive conversation wasn't her fault. It was a pre-calculated answer to an assumed question that she expected in a greeting. She didn't notice.

He spoke. He mentioned his name. Emma didn't catch it.

"I'm Emma."

He continued. After five minutes of what Emma knew to be well-rehearsed dialogue, she had a date with the dashing, young man.

The only thing different about tonight was an unscheduled shower. He arrived to her apartment at eight. She met him outside, and after a small greeting she walked straight to the bus stop. He had a car, but she didn't know this. He stood next to her without question, awaiting their public limousine.

They went to a comedy club. He disapproved of the act. The hysteria of the audience only increased his contempt for the show. He pointed out each discomfort that the theatre had to offer, and walked out thoroughly unsatisfied and out of sixty dollars.

Emma knew that the show had been contrived and bland. She realized the general infancy of the crowd that adored it only highlighted a lost cause. This train of thought was second nature to her enlightenment, but she could not stand her date's comments—it was only blowing air into the emptiness inside of her.

They barely talked during dinner. The food was okay. He nervously swirled his wine, cupped in his hand.

"Ignorance is most definitely bliss, but bliss is beyond all doubt thinner than this cheap alcohol," he said. Turns out someone actually talked like that.

Emma had no idea what he was saying, but her dinner wasn't filling her up anymore. She forced a laugh to show her expected agreement.

He swirled the glass even more violently than before. The deep red liquid stretched its way over the brim and onto his faded, yellow shirt. "Oh, great! I was gonna wear this tomorrow." He nearly threw his wine back onto the table, spilling more onto the restaurant's pristinely whitened tablecloth.

Emma shifted in her chair and offered in a cheerful tone, "Oh well. You can just wear another one. That'll come out." She knew immediately treating it with club soda and then doubled time in the washer would take care of it, but she didn't tell him. The cleaning secret made her smile, which she quickly wiped away once she realized that he was doing the same.

The next day, Emma decided to see her brother. She always knew where to find him now. He was in the hospital.

"Hey, dude." Her conversation was always much more relaxed around him.

"What up, sis?" He forced a weak smile.

Emma awkwardly glanced around the room for a seat.

He patted the edge of his bed, and laughed in a succession of coughs. "Welcome to my humble abode." It was attacking his immune system pretty efficiently now.

"Nice … nice." She wasn't good at this. She knew there wasn't much to say. "You see the last episode?" She was ready with some quotes to volley with.

Her dying brother winced. "Ah, I missed it."

"Oh … " Emma tapped her feet on the floor.

The heart monitor beeped in good rhythm.

Her brother joined in with clicks of his tongue, then quick, successive beeps of his call button.

Emma, now standing and performing a self-taught style of tap dancing in tennis shoes, rapped on the bedpan with two pens. Her brother mechanically raised and lowered his electronic bed—his best possible version of the robot dance, and much more literal.

The symphony made them both smile—not a forced grin, or a disguised grimace—real smiles.

"What the heck is going on in here?" A rushing nurse scolded them with a dramatic punch to the call button to turn it off. "Come on now, you know better, Miss Emma."

Emma smiled to her brother. "Sorry, bro."

Her brother responded with a gnarly sign hoisted above his head.

The nurse continued. "Well, you two. I have a third band member for you. There's a pretty young lady here to see you, Michael. I'll send her in."

Despite her abstinence from most of cable, Emma relished her brother's love life like a TV drama romance. "Which one?"

Michael gravely shook his head.

"Oh." Emma was already up and getting her things together.

Michael motioned back to the end of the bed. "You don't have to–"

"Hi." It was her.

Emma scooped the rest of her belongings as her demeanor changed without warning. "Okay, well—good seeing you, dude. Mom'll be in later." She hunched her back to the weight of her bags and bent her head with the burden of an assumed embarrassment that lacked a real cause, and twitched a passing smile to her brother's visitor who didn't even attempt a polite objection to Emma's motivated departure.

Days and nights passed. Movie after movie, dinner after dinner, and Emma continued to leave her suitor hanging in the main lobby. She was not happy. His negativity during each date increased all the while believing he and Emma were becoming closer. They were not. She was indeed confused by his company to her lobby following each prosaic rendezvous: she was safe once she got inside of her building and his extra precautions seemed pretty ridiculous.

Realization took some time: *Oh. He wanted to come in—all the way in—with her.* This time marked the end of their ninth date as Emma turned her back to his final, lingering "good-bye" attempt at entry, and closed the door. Ignorant insult was then added to the young man's hidden injury with the click of the deadbolt.

Tuesdays were impossible to avoid. No matter how much she tried to ignore his call after a previous date, all the cubicles in the world couldn't keep him from asking her out on these days of lesson planning.

"How about just some coffee tonight? I know a place. It's not *too* dreadful." He always left before she could answer, and relayed his instructions with a shout over his shoulder. "I'll pick you up at seven …"

He had a car? Emma turned back to her work. She'd plan out her night's progression later.

He always showed up on time. Emma liked that. He apologized for the poor condition of his car as they sped off to a place to which Emma did not want to go. Talk radio filled in the silence. In a different life of confidence, Emma would have insisted on some pop music, but this life only allowed her present being to passively disapprove of her purposeful apathy. She focused on the whining voices of the disgruntled hosts—she figured it was better than her date's ongoing, complacent commentary.

They sat in the back of the shop. He sipped on his "the usual" while Emma unscrewed and recapped her apple juice—a choice that went against the ridiculously upbeat and inarticulate cashier's advice to try a new mocha, frosted, hand-spun cappuccino topped with whip cream. Apparently, her date noticed this too.

"It's like she doesn't know talking only highlights her stupidity."

Emma mishandled and dropped her cap at the end of his proclamation. She squeezed her eyes and raised her eyebrows in an attempt to show sleepiness. "It's getting late. I have class tomorrow."

He cocked his head. "You mean—work?"

Emma felt a seed of panic in her temple, planted by a guilt that now swam freely through her body. "Oh, right," she blurted. "Well, it is getting late."

He smiled at Emma the way he would admire the innocence of a nervous kitten. "It is," he said. "And as work goes," he groaned, "I have it too. Such agony, huh?" Again, defying the expectancy of normally phrased conversation.

Emma allowed her response to be drowned by the apple juice she was chugging. She wouldn't let it go to waste. She thought about trying to tell him about the love and care she had for her students, and that things didn't have to be so terrible all the time. Something inside her clotted her throat, and pounded on her heart. She could not tell him how she felt about the world. She could not tell him how it felt to be trapped in the melancholy lull of life's futility, and to be in everyone's head but her own. She could not say any of these things, because he wouldn't understand, and neither would she.

As the car whizzed past the front of her apartment building, Emma made small sounds of protest, but definitely not enough of an effort that could reach him before he parked in the back lot. He walked her to the lobby, and she turned to say good bye. This is where she usually could leave him without question. This time, his improvised advances halted her.

"I'd love to finish up our talk inside." He nodded toward any apartment in eyesight. He had never been able to track Emma's exit through the precise doorway around the corner that he was now aching to follow her through.

She couldn't bring him. The Lovers would either scare him away or egg him on. He really wanted to come in. Did he want to feed her with the same fork he had used to trap his end of the Twinkie? Yes, a less classy substitute for the romantic vision of the chocolate cake stipulated by her dreams, but somebody had to put a dent in the American treats—she got two a week.

"Emma, are you okay?" he asked.

She must have been daydreaming again.

"So, how about that coffee?" he continued.

"Uh. Yeah ... sure." She diligently mimicked an excited romantic as best she could—whatever that sounded like. Why coffee? More coffee? It was the gateway to a better life, after all.

They made it to bed quicker than Emma had expected. She did not even have time to check her answering machine. He was all over her. The TV was still on. She focused on the groping. She pleaded with her body to slip away. In her head, she thought, "end scene," as the curtains would close to thousands of over-excited hands. Nothing poetic of the sort happened. She searched for the dull sensations of the moment. She never did hear her clockwork neighbors chime in.

Minutes later, Emma was lying in the same position in which she began this encounter—no worse for the wear, but no better either. She shiftily glanced around the room as if she wasn't in her own bed, in her own apartment.

Hours later, she was still in the same place. He was sleeping. There was no cake, no Twinkie, and no singular fork. He didn't even have a meaningless question for her. In fact, he hadn't moved all night. She was cold. She had never really slept naked before. All her other sexual endeavors she had treated as an experiment, and this one, just like the others, allotted no covetable results.

---

At sight of the first ray of light twisting its way through the blinds and into the room, Emma stood up. Looking down at the spot where she had been on her bed she thought, *there might as well be an imprint molded into the mattress by now*. He still hadn't moved.

The five-minute oatmeal she had grown familiar to over the past few weeks was more bland and soggier than ever this morning. The Lovers were whispering—at least they had a good night, again. The phone ring pierced through the thick aroma of body odor that wafted throughout the apartment. He groaned loud enough so that he made his point. Emma didn't hear him.

She questioned, "Hello?" It was 5:30 in the morning.

Only a couple of seconds had passed when Emma forcefully interjected, "Can I come over in a little? Everything is going to be okay." The dialogue that radiated from her mouth was completely sincere, and Emma knew it.

As she scrambled to look presentable and not smell entirely of the hideous fusion of an undeniable disagreement between their two body odors, Emma caught eyes with the mound of blankets in her bed. He was up now, begrudgingly. They stared at each other for a long time, and in some distant way, Emma felt at ease with the action of the world.

"I'll be gone before you get back," he said peacefully, extending a hand from beneath his refuge.

Emma smiled, shook it, said "Thank you," and left. She made it halfway down the hallway when she realized that she had forgotten to lock her door. She quickly turned and raced back to it.

She could hardly believe what she saw—faces to the animalistic mating, the careless whispering, and ritual gluttony. The Lovers were crying. A couple she would never be ready to meet was standing right next to her, unaware of Emma's presence. Emma turned the bolt into the wall.

The man outside the neighboring doorframe heaved, as if he was being forced to say it—"I'm sorry, but I need something more . . . and I have to find it."

Suddenly, Emma appreciated and savored every mindless quote that had passed through the thin walls of her apartment. This was the first stupid thing she had ever heard either of them say. Emma and the sobbing male half of the entity that she had most recently labeled as *love*—loud, over-exaggerated, visceral ecstasy—left the building together. His ex-partner propped her door open, and wailed until the entire neighborhood woke.

He held the door for Emma. She thanked him and walked outside. It was a quiet day, but brighter than usual. The forgotten leaves of springtime on the ground looked to be frozen by time, a mosaic of deep red, burnt orange, and spots of yellow that proudly consumed the remaining green in each leave's veins. "Looks like rain today," the disproved lover said.

It had been a day of disrupted schedules, and Emma had not even noticed. She was in the car when it happened. The rain was pouring down the windshield, offering a thick layer of unbroken water, and distorting the view of the other cars that swished past. Everything was clear now. She ran her fingers down through her thick, brown hair, and comforted her soft cheeks with the smoothness of each lock. Her rouge lips forgot how to purse, and drifted open to allow an easy exhale. The paleness of her skin was now pure and warm as she gently brought each arm to rest on the other atop her midsection. The muscles that furrowed her thin eyebrows and wrinkling forehead relaxed, along with every other muscle that usually tensed a body that had been perfectly toned by a daily regiment of stress and anxiety. Her arms took to her flowing hair again, this time guiding it behind her, and revealing artistically rounded shoulders and a long, elegant neck that journeyed to the undeniable beauty that stemmed from it. The complex painting of Emma was captured in her oceanic blue, crystallized eyes, which now rested in a sedated, content gaze, looking for nothing in particular, since Emma had already found it.

It had been three days. Emma was sitting on the back of the bus, peacefully daydreaming. It stopped, and she realized that she had made that specific request. She and her refined knapsack made their way through the calm sea of people and stepped off the bus. As she began her way to the curb, she turned around. She thought she heard the bus driver say something to her—too late. It was already revving its engine and continuing its route. It would be back. She noticed the passing, but immobilized faces as the bus made its repetitive departure. The male lover, who Emma had finally been able to match a face to, was staring right at her. He looked miserable.

Returning to her promenade toward her apartment, she stepped in a puddle. It still hadn't dried up from a couple days earlier of rain. Her small, quiet bits of laughter rose from deep in her chest. She was wearing rain boots for the first time that week. Wind tore the wet leaves from the pavement and created a swirling pathway to the main lobby for Emma. She walked purposefully, but not without appreciation for each heel-toe she experienced. Her parents were coming over for dinner. The whole family was—minus one.

"Hey, Mom," Emma answered her phone. "How are you? ... No, of course. Come over whenever ... Yeah, I figured no one would be too hungry. I'll throw it on the stove in a little anyways—no big deal ... Okay, love you. See you soon. Tell Dad I'm putting the game on too. K, bye." Emma hung up, turned a thoughtful smile, and stood still to feel the trail of moisture. She knowingly allowed a small tear to gently journey down the side of her cheek. Everything was going to be okay.

*The first side effect of pain is real, unadulterated, rational thought, not to be confused with the processed, cultivated, regimented idealism of those caught in the reverberations of this pain. Onlookers go beyond the suffering—plan for the future, seek long-term treatment, and empathize, through pity, as much as possible. Those who suffer, cope. They endlessly seek immediate relief, constantly assess the support around them as useful, superfluous, or even damaging. Rather than hope for the best, they avoid the worst.*

# part 2

## *potential*

"I do."

This was real time. It was no painful flashback and no luminous premonition. It was death do they part. Maddie sucked in and bit the insides of her cheeks, tasting the blood of her anxiety. She shuttered to the three strands of hair that interrupted her gaze, unable to fully recognize the groom's intently focused, optic stream of love toward the beautiful wonder that stood so close. Her blonde hair gracefully flowed downward in intricate curls. They shaped her head like a golden aura and gently unraveled onto her shoulders. In between breaths, Maddie brushed back the renegade hairs that were silhouetted by the beam of sunlight that was shooting through a missing piece of stained glass, and appropriately spotlighting this earthly angel dressed in all white.

Her arms quickly resumed a rigid position at the waist, frightened by their sudden movement. Her hands desperately gripped each other, as if they alone held the two halves of the body together, constantly interlocking and rearranging their bony fingers, spiraled by the veins that visibly pulsed in anticipation. She didn't understand. As a kid, teenager, young adult, and now woman she had always been independent, intelligent, witty, beautiful—enough to make the man next to her lucky to land such a girl. Her unblemished cheeks swelled below her catlike eyes—green and sharp—each eyeball sitting in deep sockets carved by dark, defining creases that added to the deepening pull of the jaded irises. The bride lowered her eyelashes to shade the unintentional intimidation of her scathing glare, and half-smiled to her fiancé's jaw-clenching grin.

She always said that she would never marry—she had too much to accomplish. Yet having a man by her side definitely validated all these gifts and beauties that she had claimed. To her, she was getting older, losing confidence, and the next man in her life might be the last. She made it so. There wasn't much thought to it—her life, with a male accessory.

Now, Maddie had this disorder that caused her to live in every time but the present. She did learn from her mistakes, but never had time to practice the right judgment at which she had previously failed. She was looking ahead to the future—not that she didn't know it; it wouldn't have a name if she didn't know what it was. She knew exactly what was going to happen in life—she, Maddie Malone, was going to be happy. Yet, there she was, dressed in white (she hated herself in white. Everyone knew that dark green was her color), already struggling to remember the eloquence of her vows.

"You may kiss the bride."

As she withdrew her lips from her husband's face, whose eyes remained closed and lips frozen in kiss, Maddie retreated to her heels, and padded her fashionably restricted diaphragm.

Shotgun on right side of the bed.

*Tink tink. Tink tink.* Dad was giving a toast. Maddie caught only bits and pieces of it. "The only girl who hates some things as much as I do…"

"…She sat on the swing and her smile would melt you. Anyone just arriving to the scene wouldn't know that as a six-year-old, she had just picked out every single psychological and physical flaw I had at the moment. She was smiling at how smart she knew she was."

Maddie hid the same smile under her napkin, catching the undercooked carrots she was happily coughing out. This wedding could have used a better caterer.

Raising his glass, Jack continued. "Eat up everyone, but not too loud. You know how that bothers us…"

He wasn't finished, but Maddie's attention faded into passive frustration as her father chimed back in. He was a good father, and there was a down payment on her new house to prove it. She was satisfied. Tonight was about her—that would explain the severe lack of fun she experienced as she moved throughout the sea of well-wishers. No matter, her brother looked great. She couldn't believe he stayed on his feet so long. He unintentionally stole the carefree, one-night-only, no responsibility feeling supposedly gifted to most newlyweds in preparation for a hotel suite for two people, one vacation, and two obvious but somewhat suddenly, very different agendas.

Maddie's mind drifted to her and her husband's arrival to their suite. She would want to do this. *He* would want sex. She would suggest a show of some sort. He would suggest his standing ovation. She liked sitting silently under the moonlight. This gave him too many ideas. Hopefully this thing didn't last forever.

Maddie's obsessed projection of the future continued throughout the night. Her first dance was the two hundredth time it had been danced by her and her husband, and all she could see was their two hundred and twenty fifth rehearsal at their five-year anniversary. Looping melodies of clicking champagne flutes occupied the forthcoming memory of dinner with friends that did not yet occur, on an aged, oak dining table that did not yet exist, within the walls of a deep-rouge room that was not yet painted. The smaller children in the great hall flickered across the dance floor, and the bride looked on with a brewing intensity of impatience—her eyes, vacuums of the joy that surrounded her; a motivated greed for the populated joys of life and thus a tragic incapacity to experience them.

Maddie's detailed visions that breached the abilities of a clairvoyant were interrupted as she burst into laughter and rewound to her ongoing wedding reception, grabbing her father-in-law's shoulder and simulating an over-acted fan with her hand. The light was strongly reflected off her new, shiny band, and hit her father-in-law in the eye. His confused face tightened into a severe pile of kneaded cookie dough. "That wasn't even the punch-line," he said with a dismissive giggle.

They met in their last year of college. Everyone knew Maddie, and nobody knew him. She made a regular entrance into a party, and with a flick of her head, swooping her long, blonde hair to the side, she parted the messy gathering of drunken students as she made her way to the kitchen. It's not that she asked for any of the attention, but it seemed that this particular boy had not gotten the memo. He stood talking to what was presumably a possible candidate for a coed sleepover that he was attempting to arrange, and Maddie, in her heels, was not about to journey the extra three feet around him to enter the kitchen.

"Excuse me." Oh no! She sounded like a stuck-up, prissy high schooler that did nothing but sit around, gossip about her classmates, and paint her finger nails.

He barely gave her a look of recognition, lifting up his drink to signify that Maddie had to squeeze through.

"I bet she has a different color to paint her finger nails with every day." He knew Maddie heard him, as she stepped through the bi-gender sandwich. She physically shrugged off the public comment, but keeping her nose in the air didn't keep her eyes off of him for the rest of the night.

She finally found him alone on the couch, more than a few drinks (and shouts of "Chug!") into the night.

"Hi." Maddie sat a cushion apart from the slouching victim of the weekend.

"Hey... meany pants." It wasn't a matured wit by any means, but it was enough insult paired with flirt to rope her in.

She rolled her eyes at his drunken savvy. "I know," Maddie cutely raised her voice like a slide whistle. "That's why I wanted to apologize. Like my nails?" She waved them obnoxiously in his face.

"Funny. But yes I do. They're very pretty—match your eyes." He had a weak smile to show for it. Maddie's nails were blue. It was his confidence in something that was absolutely wrong that charmed her, and his soothing sincerity that made her forget what color her eyes really were.

She dropped her head in a shy manner. For some reason his failed attempts at cat and mouse were charming. "I'm self-conscious. I'm sorry. You have no idea how much I worry about stuff like this." She pointed to her hair (untouched for four hours now) and then to her nails. "I usually say everything twice over in my head before it actually comes out..." Why was she telling him this? Was he even listening?

He shook his head slowly, because going too fast would make him nauseous. "No. You're beautiful, and smart, and funny, and... and you said sorry... and pretty." He had not even learned her name yet, didn't know her, and could most likely barely make out a clear picture of her face. "No more worrying." He aimed for her forehead and got her eyelid, kissed it, and sat back to rest on the couch after his effort. He offered his arm to shield her from all judgment, fear, doubt, and failure in the world. She took it. She rested the side of her head on his chest like a hunter to the ground, listening carefully for any vibration. She felt inexplicably safe as the thumps of his heart steadied her breathing and cleared her mind.

He walked her to her apartment that night, and laughing, they agreed that he would call "M-a-d-d-i-e… don't forget!" the next morning. The drunken gentlemen walked off into the horizon, whistling an improvised melody and taking back all the security he had given to Maddie that night home with him. She'd wait all night for the call the next morning.

---

It took until three in the afternoon for Maddie's phone to buzz with an unnamed number. It was him, and she was already mad. However, throughout their entire courtship Maddie did not once scold him for his absentmindedness, his tardiness, or his subsequent ignorance of his selfishness. She made do—she needed his confidence, and she ached for his shelter. She closed her eyes for the rest. If this was love, she wasn't going to work any harder for something else she didn't need. He would help her along her road to happiness.

Nonetheless, the road was bumpy, and Maddie inconveniently added roadblocks of preconceived expectations. She wasn't sure what they were, but he most certainly was not fulfilling them.

Ironically, many of their nights out were likened to the first time they met—for him at least. He would tell her how happy he was, and before she could begin to concoct an answer (which on most nights would dodge the truth or be a flat out lie) he would kiss her, swallowing Maddie's growing sadness. Good nights came, rarely, and the bad nights (for Maddie) continued until one date, he began the night's end on one knee. Whether it was Maddie's fear of the unknown or the complacency of a "sure thing," or the fact that she had long been convinced that the man in front of her filled in the gaps in her character, it didn't matter—Maddie was getting married. She loved him so much that night, and for many months after. "Marriage" seemed to be a magic word.

The world was right in front of them, and she knew that they could snatch it and put it in the palm of her hand. But first, she was going to change it. Maddie was a product of contemporary, projected idealism of a feigned compassion and goodwill, justified by a passive selfishness, feeling entitled to an expected life of proper reward. Not that she didn't think teaching was worthwhile, or that her fifteen dollars a month to the Gates' foundation was futile—these parts of her life were necessary, to reinforce the qualities that people commended, respected, adored. A means to an end, a sensible path. Her reality was a conceptual idea, and depended on the assessment of others. In such a way, worth was tangible; happiness was concrete. She believed in this, and he believed in her.

"Good morning, my wife." The man next to her in bed softly whispered into her ear while tucking behind it her tangled hair, still scented by her shampoo. "I dreamt that I was sleeping next to you last night. It was a perfect dream, and when I woke up, it only got better."

The inseparable pair worked together at a local public school. Maddie's kids were the perfect juxtaposition to her ongoing standard of what the future had to offer. She and her husband would have their own child some day, but for the moment, Maddie lived and loved in the present.

It was a morning when the drapes that covered the window successfully delegated a reasonable compromise with the stubborn, searing attitude of the rising sun, as they collectively dimmed its dutiful charge into the retreating darkness of the bedroom. Once its subdued rays had slowly raised its subjects' eyelids, the yawning individuals were instantaneously grateful for waking in such a comfortable bed, taking in a calm breath of air. The bedroom was painted gold by the sun's softened light, and gently welcomed the couple to ease into the day. The two hosted a breakfast in bed, appreciating each minute that edged closer to the fulfilling day ahead of them. They kissed—her strawberry flavored lips overlapping with his, still white from the whipped cream. It was going to be a good day.

Maddie spent each day waiting to see him again. Any trouble or problem she had became weightless at his touch. When she looked into his eyes, everything in this world (and any other world for that matter) made sense. There were no questions, and only answers.

On a spring night, as the moon gave its full attention to their bedroom window while they lay next to each other, smiling—just because—it was time to extend the boundaries of their love. Sleep was not necessary that night, nor was it missed in the least.

Six weeks later, Maddie earnestly locked gaze with her husband's eyes from the observation chair. She knew nothing could come between them as he whistled a soft melody to relax her eyelids.

"And do you see that small flicker?" The doctor motioned toward a small monitor to Maddie's left. "That, Mrs. and Mr. Geraghty, is a heartbeat."

Maddie pulled from her husband's entranced stare. She blindly grabbed the first thing she could find on him as she looked at the tiny picture of a growing fetus. She tightened her grasp on his pant-leg as his puckered lips became lost for whistle. The doctor knew not to speak, stepping back to admire the picturesque affection that the couple was displaying.

Maddie's stomach got bigger as the months quickly passed, and so did the couple's devotion. They were going to name him William, per tradition. The walls were painted a delicate blue in the newly furnished nursery, equipped with every comfort and technology available for a new family member. Everything and everyone was ready.

Maddie's husband never left her side. Each morning, he woke up an hour early to cook breakfast, lay out her clothes, ready the shower, and patiently wait in the warming car (practically on top of their doorstep). During school, he organized his eighth graders to become "big brothers and sisters" to her second graders. At night, he massaged her back until she drifted off to the classical music (for the baby—Maddie read somewhere that it was good fetal therapy). He found little time to rest as he watched his beautiful wife peacefully dream of the approaching years of their lives. For him, each wakeful minute that passed only increased his complete, fulfilling, and blissful devotion to her. He refused to acknowledge the failure of his drooping eyelids as they blocked the sight of his love, and ignorantly fell into a tentative sleep.

"Hey! Wake up! I think it's time ..." She flooded him with kisses all over his face. Each piercing contraction only made Maddie more ecstatic. They rushed to the hospital, Maddie smiling and hugging her husband's hand, not giving it back to him even as the wheelchair dizzily rolled to the emergency room by a one-handed steering effort.

"Sir ... Sir! Please, sir!" Nursing schools dedicate a few words of advice in calming concerned relatives of a patient. They never helped.

"My wife's in there! She's in there! She needs me! Need to be in there!"

"Sir!" The nurse was practically hugging at his waist as he dragged her out of the waiting room. "Rick! ... Some help?"

The whole staff wouldn't be able to hold him back. He broke free of their grips and raced into the hallways, just in time to see Maddie being wheeled out of her room by a swarm of bloody doctors.

"Madeline!"

She had seen him, and her arm was already stretched out beyond the hurrying bodies that surrounded her bed.

He grabbed it, rushing after the rolling bed, like he was desperately trying to escape onto the caboose of a moving train with the help of an already boarded passenger. What he said was barely audible, as the shouts of the doctors created a bubble of terror over Maddie. "I love you. Everything's going to be okay. I'm here." Let that be enough, please.

The bed crashed through the swinging doors of the O.R. The posse of nurses had caught up to the action by now, stepping in front of his entry.

"You cannot go in there, sir!" A scared young girl just out of med school.

"They will take care of her! You just can't go in the operating room, man. It's not safe." A man on his thirteenth hour of his shift.

"We can talk you through it, but right now, they need to save the baby, sir." An impossibly chipper woman who had obviously joined this field of work for the psychological value.

He couldn't hear any of them. He slowly lost the grip of his wife's hand, finger by finger, as he was pushed back into the hallway. She wasn't crying. She wasn't struggling. Her eyes were wide open, staring at his. He cried. He didn't have any more answers for her. He just wanted her to be okay.

Three hours had passed and Maddie was now unconscious, in bed, and under the heavy surveillance of her doctors. She was going to live. Her husband stood outside of her room with a hand over his pursed mouth as he listened to her head doctor, all the while refusing to break his watch on his immobile wife.

"We couldn't save the baby, Mr. Geraghty. I am sorry," he spoke direct and objectively. "The baby's heart was weakening and the umbilical cord was too tightly wound around his neck. By the time we got to him—it was too late. I'm sorry. Your wife will have to stay here for a few nights, but she's going to be fine." He shook the patient's spouse's hand, apologized again, and strode off to his next patient. Maddie was going to live, but she was not going to be fine. Her husband sat next to her, trying to will their love's survival.

Watching life through a dirty window.
Stupor. Alonecoldconfused. Horror. hys-
tericsrestraintsedated. Disconnected.
Panicsshockconvulsionscrippled. Fetus. Child.
William. Desolatedespairbrokenhelplessresentment.
Ghost. Angerdepressionrejectioncrumblingforfeit.
Tears. Staggered Breath. Hatred.
Deflatedshriveledburstflooded-
drownedsuffocatedpossessedexorcised. Therapy.
Celexaprozaclithiumcymbaltazoloftnembutal. Flowers.
Tombstone. Vicodinpercocetcodeineoxycodone. Therapy.

Husbandloverantagonistignorant-
judgmentalguiltless. Denial.
Emptinessstretchedoutofreachdetached *William*.
Awake. Comatose. Alive. Programmed.
Sleepmorningbreakfastgymdoctor-
pilllunchsleepmoviefamilydinnerfightd-
enypillsleep. Age. Deteriorate. Distance.
Featurestoesfirststepwordeyebrows-
fingernailsnaptimetimeoutkindergartenhomework-
graduationfriendstalentspassionmotherhood. Lost.

Suddenly, everything in life was no longer a validation of hope, a confirmation of being, a beckoning of an omniscient smile—as if all that had occurred in the world had fallen like dominoes in order to bow to a particular moment or succumb to, by all other means, a nonsensical realization. The charm of life was no more than a trail of seduction that birthed its most prized possessions of reality—hurt, terror, suffering, impurity, hopelessness. The unknown.

The parental wind that combs the soft, budding hair of an infant. The calming pervasiveness of a tepid stream of water that runs down each finger as a newer, more pure skin, not yet singed by heat, and too content to anticipate the treacherous betrayal of cold. Inhale spring's first breath of fresh air. Find a sincere, noble star fighting to stay visible in a city's navy blue sky on a night when the streetlights have grown tired and the chirping of crickets prevails over the distant wailing of an ambulance and disapproving car horns. When faith discounts reason. Close one eye, and touch the horizon. To love. To use eyes to speak with a closed mouth, and to synchronize two beating hearts without knowing how. To grow in union, to have child.

The first scent of a rose, and the bitter scorn for its first winter. Happy Second Birthday, William.

---

Maddie wasn't sure how to feel anymore. Maybe today was just a renewal of her depression, since the only thing that had faded was the physical proof of her loss. She slid her hands over the cloth of her pants and onto the covered scar tissue. She didn't want to forget.

The apartment door opened, then shut. No whistle today, not for a while. Her husband peeked into the bedroom to find his wife staring straight at him. So naturally, he flexed his biceps. "Hey, baby." *Two hours at the gym every day after work still wasn't enough,* Maddie thought. Her eyes were always open now.

"What's for din din?" He knew that she hated silly abbreviations for common words, but almost everyone disagreed with a greeting stare, which was quickly turning into a glare, a class three stare. He avoided eye contact by conducting a nasal combing of his entire body, in search of the origin of the odor that his presence had gifted the apartment.

"What are you feeling tonight, honey?" Like it mattered. She knew he caught her thick sarcasm. The next words that came out of his mouth had better be chosen wisely.

He tip-toed to a long, drawn out—"Well . . . I thought I could take you out on a hot date tonight. Dinner, movie . . . " and biting his lower lip and surveying his wife like a new girl that he had just met at the bar, "And possibly, you know, relations of any possible . . . " he stepped close and raked his hands through her hair, "sexual adventures." He wanted to clap for his own performance.

"Ugh. I'll get dressed I guess." She dodged his attempts at a kiss. "And you . . . not that orange shirt." She left him halfway to pursing his lips. He opened his overflowing closet with a sigh. He knew the contract was void without her signature.

"No. You don't get how selfish you are?" Maddie and her husband walked in the door after their impromptu date. He was wearing the orange shirt (now with a blotch of spaghetti to complement the florescent background), and his face looked so shocked one would think he had been staring at the neon cloth all night instead of the movie.

"Whaat? Are you talking about? The things that I did tonight? Was really fun I thought!" It was like some weird game where he began each new sentence with the final word from his last exclamation.

Maddie would point out the literary flaws in his disassociated argument later. Her blurts of rage when walking through the door were just the beginning of the fight. She usually fast-forwarded the earlier conversations and key mistakes of her husband in her mind, and he never could catch up. It was like *Minority Report*, but less fair.

"If you didn't even want to go out tonight, why did you even ask me?" Maddie quickly threw in the bait.

He actually had had fun, and thought she had too. But it didn't matter—he knew this game. He must have done something wrong, and recalling it or trying to fix it was not what Maddie wanted. He put on his gloves. He wouldn't need his mouthpiece—all his teeth had already been knocked out. "You were the one who couldn't manage a decent meal for the two of us!"

"That's because I know my fat, sack of a husband doesn't need it!"

They went all twelve rounds.

"Here! This is how you wanted the night to end, right?" She unbuttoned her shirt. One last chance for her so-called husband.

He retreated into a nearby chair, focusing hard on the folded hands in his lap like a monster who just discovered the terror of his ways. The other beast was still breathing heavily, showing a cleavage that dared the man to look.

He advanced one step at a time with his hands out and his head slightly turned as if averting his eyes from a raging fire but still desperately seeking the warmth and beauty it had to offer. "Honey, look. Please. I love you. I'm sorry." He tried placing his hands on her shoulders, instinctively trying to keep her in place. He touched her arm.

"You're disgusting," she coldly whispered. "Good night, dear." She briskly strode to the bedroom, threw out a blanket and pillow in no particular direction, and whisked the door shut. The pillow had landed near her husband, who was standing frozen in the hallway, disgusted with the hand that attempted human contact. He looked up and saw the closed entry to his bedroom, and drifted to the living room couch. A single tear fought its way down his face, zigzagging to the chin, and slowly stretching its body into a freefall, landing next to another wet puddle on the pillow.

The haunted father focused on the two drying blotches of the same drowning heartbreak for a long time. "I miss him, too," he whispered.

Maddie sat upright in the bed amid a classic scene of a pillow fortress protecting her, a box of tissues comforting her, and a concerned childhood doll counseling her. She was humiliated in the presence of nobody, and was nervous in front of an audience of inanimate objects. She was so unhappy. She was still an uninspired teacher who could never pass a student in her class without guilt. Then again, nothing came without guilt. She hated herself for every bite of food she took. The family she had was always an obligatory phone call away. Everything was a game without a high score, and Maddie was convinced that she had run out of cheat codes. Even her marriage was a match of Pong. Each day the ball was getting faster, and she and her husband continued to alternate whacks at it, keeping it in play. This wasn't what she wanted. This wasn't happiness. She fell asleep fast; she always did. She'd have to remind herself to get a refill on the bottle of Nembutal hidden in her nightstand.

The next day, Maddie woke up at 6:59. She hovered her palm over the snooze button for the next hour of a minute. Seven o'clock and—*click. That* was satisfying control. She rolled over and cuddled up next to the warm body of her husband. He was still wearing the orange shirt. She kissed his forehead, and he stirred with a smile. She was glad he came back.

"Time for school," he murmured. They were both teachers, uninspired and energetic, respectively—Maddie being most responsible for the former.

She pointed to the wall with both fingers excitedly, confusing her groggy, tangerine husband. "Things your wife doesn't care about... Ding ding ding! You win!" She put her hands back on his chest.

"What did I win?" No Family Feud contestant had ever mischievously smiled to the host like the present participant, but then again, this wasn't a game. Maddie didn't want to go to school today. Make the calls. No school today.

The sick-day proved to be one for the ages. Food was ordered, movies were watched, and the momentary love was made. They did nothing, and enjoyed everything. After his shower, fully clothed in the latest sporting attire, the husband knelt down in front of Maddie.

"I love you."

"You're cute. Go work out," the rejuvenated wife said, while licking the chocolate sauce off his cheek that he had shoddily missed in his two-minute shower.

"You know it, baby! Gotta keep this bod in tip-top shape for days like this with you. See you in a little," he framed her from a few feet away with his L-formed hands (they didn't have a camera—Maddie hated pictures). "Perfect."

"Bye," the temporary model batted her eyelashes. The door closed, and muffled the whistling she so often dreaded. It usually approached the door from a long day's work in the next few minutes, but it was leaving this time. She would miss it dearly.

Maddie woke up the next morning with no recollection of yesterday's happiness or reason for its occurrence, and felt only its consequences. She was bloated, felt entirely unaccomplished, and sustained a headache only fit to follow a six-pack of Mountain Dew and enough beef jerky to feed a class of eight-year-old boys—most of whom would be waiting in homeroom twenty-five minutes from now. Without a word, she tore out of bed (she hated the left side) and raced into the bathroom.

"Good morning, Beautiful. I thought I'd let you sleep in—you deserved it."

Maddie had no breath to counter the stammering idiocracies coming from her husband, who apparently wanted nothing more than to make her life harder.

The car ride to school was like a one-night stand the morning after, with no memory of formal introductions. He knew she was mad, how could he not? All the things he does to her. He pulled in front of the main doors.

"I'm sor–" Maddie slammed the car door behind her before he could finish. On her break, she sat in a bathroom stall to silently sob, bite her fist, then open the door to a student on a "bathroom emergency."

"Oh hi, Lucy! See you in class... don't forget most people in third world countries don't have running water for luxuries that include nice bathrooms like this." Lucy was in Maddie's Social Studies class. Today was really bad. She'd take two pills tonight.

Spring break began, and the morning drive, the couple's last dependable session of unavoidable quality time, ended. Her husband would get up early to exercise, and Maddie would set out to visit her brother with her husband's counterfeit, best wishes. It didn't matter—she wasn't going to mention her husband during her time with her afflicted brother anyways. He was admitted to inpatient care during her last visit home—only she might return home, her brother would not, save a miracle or less likely, a sudden advancement in treatment for his condition.

The visits weren't helping either of them, and Maddie found herself getting lost for no apparent reason on her way back to her apartment each afternoon. She always felt different after a visit to her brother. Worse—like her problems were locked up inside of her and attacking her insides when she saw him.

One day she drove right past the hospital. She just kept driving. When she finally got home, she had the place to herself. She began lesson planning for the next semester that was just days away. This is what she did—lesson planning. She felt like taking the rest of her pills. A tune to no particular song came into earshot. It was the whistling, God forbid. As the door opened, the whistling was interrupted by Maddie's mother's voice.

"Is Mads home?" she asked her son-in-law.

"Yeah. I think so." He called, "Maddie … you home? Your mom's here. Wanted to tell us something."

The conversation was over, and Maddie's mom went for the door. Maddie wanted to say something. She stood up and opened her mouth, but her mother was gone. Tears toppled down her cheeks. For the first time, she couldn't make out what the future was going to bring. She couldn't see it at all; she was blinded by the present. Any control in life that she demanded was now lost.

Maddie's husband reached for her shoulder, and this time took hold of it. He pulled her in and tightened his grasp. He put his other hand around her head, burying her tears into his shirt. He whispered to her, "Everything is gonna be all right. You hear me?" She looked at him like it was the first time she had ever seen his face. Bill was his name. Her husband's name was Bill.

*In layman's terms, pain is suddenly no longer just pain. It becomes a package deal, complete with reckless behavior and inescapable depression. It hates our gifts and abilities and feeds off our weaknesses.*

# part 3

## *intimacy*

Acting never happened—Jack was too nervous on stage (wisdom entrusted to him by an audience to his vomiting during a collegiate performance of Hans Christian Anderson). A screenplay could have worked, but the paranoia of failure swallowed every drama, comedy, and tragedy whole—down to the typed-written credits of Jack's eleven font-sized name. He would have been a critic of some sort, but the vocalization of his doubts, theories, and suggestions always seemed to come at only the wrong times. Instead, Jack was making an agreeable salary as a writer for a mid-level, political magazine. A novelist he was not—published at least—but this did not stop the past middle-aged man from painfully scribbling in a twenty-year-old notepad about the adventures of a young boy who dreamed of being an astronaut. Ironically, Jack gave that dream up mid-way through his high school career—the moon was too far from everyone he loved.

Despite a steady job, an equally steady income, a familiar residence, and enough luxuries to satisfy any man, Jack could not stop panicking. It was a nonstop anxiety, like a little boy sitting on the stoop waiting for his birthday package. The brown box of fulfilled dreams never arrived at Jack's doorstep, but he was too afraid to stop waiting. Each stage in his life was a room to which he was too cautious to close the door because he knew he had forgotten something.

He loved his family with all his heart, despite their inevitable and understandably unintentional addition to his worries. This frustrated him. Anything unplanned caused too much stress, and no one understood. He idly witnessed the same symptoms course through his daughter's thoughts and rampage all her days of sunshine. This frustrated him more. He *had* to make money for his family; he *needed* to raise his kids right; he could not fail them. In turn, respect, obedience, and affection *must* be shown to the selfless father and husband, though of course he knew this idea of symbiotic love was never certain.

Nothing was ever certain—it had become Jack's silent mantra that hummed ever so loudly throughout most of his life. Maybe it was his drunk of a father, but truthfully, the physical beatings never bothered him beyond occasionally favoring a leg or avoiding an extra bump to a bruise. It was the lack of emotional care that most likely did all the damage, as his mother continually displayed her annoyed negligence day in and day out throughout his childhood. No matter the path that chose him, Jack now regularly fidgeted in bed most of every night, over-acting each flail of the body, and clearly articulating each disapproval for any creak, clatter, or voice box within earshot. He was aware that his maladies antagonized any glimpse of rest his wife had, but Jack was trapped in his own prison.

It wasn't bad all the time. For a grounded man who grew up in poverty, Jack had grown fairly accustomed to the plasma TV (nearly a member of the family) just beyond his bed, frequent fine-dining paired with an accessible wallet that could solve most problems, and the four-star hotels that warmly welcomed him when he arrived on business (an act of humility according to Jack, who attested to the unnecessary accommodations of a five-star). Life was almost always good, but Jack wasn't.

It's not that he wasn't grateful, and as the previously described husband and father, he loved his family with every ounce of energy that he woke with each day. But at war, Jack could not pledge allegiance to anyone, including himself. The father in him strove to protect and raise his children so that they might *painlessly* walk though life, but Jack despised any handout he gave them and mourned the love that he claimed was never given in return. The husband in him was utterly selfless in every way, with wishes of fulfilling the needs, wants, and desires of his wife. Yet Jack could not help but manifest a growing frustration and malcontent, consequence of a selfless act that reaped no personal benefit. It was a sincere conflict of self, heightened by the common ego and personal preference that bred ignorant selfishness.

—

"Hellooo!" Jack always entered the house in a 1950s TV-sitcom fashion. For having such a large head, most of his facial requirements—retreating eyes, protruding nose, thin lips, and emaciated cheeks—were confined to a very small oval below his growing forehead (whatever hair he had left was kept to a close buzz, giving a shade of grey to the shine of his baldness). His unnaturally thin eyebrows hovered above his slumped brow, as if he was in constant surprise, while his faded brown eyes bounced from side to side in accordance.

He waited, burnishing his around-the-clock five o'clock shadow. "I'm home!" Of course he was—he always prepared his arrival with a ring of the doorbell as he fished for his keys. His withered hands sprang from his pockets, revealing his twisted fingers and open palms that were left only with dulling discoloration, reminiscent of forgotten calluses.

"Hey, Hon! Upstairs!" His wife Kathryn never followed the rules of the sitcom—it was hard to pose on the banister of the stairwell with a kid in each arm. Dad and Husband understood, but Jack still wished a smiling face had greeted him.

Jack was left behind as the father and husband rushed upstairs, three at a time by his skeletal legs, to over-excitedly engage his restless children, and exhausted wife. The husband magnetically drew eyes with his beautiful wife and froze time with a genuine expression of love and happiness. Every muscle in his face relaxed, his lower lip dropped, and his mouth stayed half-open in a way that said a thousand words of romance as speechlessness arrested him. His pupils dilated then tightened like a camera lens working for perfect clarity. The woman that had bore two of his kids with a third on the way was a natural wonder of beauty, wisdom, and love. The bills didn't matter; his kids were amazing. His body and mind were deaf to the white noise that surrounded him. He was lost in a dream, and found in heaven.

The clock hand ticked forwards another six degrees, alerting the room that another second had passed. Time resumed, and Jack, regaining consciousness, took his throne above the suffocating father and husband. "Anything for dinner tonight? You know how much I love your cooking." It was a sarcastic blow to the burnt chicken marsala he was treated to the night before, but said in a loving manner—enough to only incite a harmless eye-roll from his wife. Jack worked all day, and he was hungry.

The third child had arrived—a boy, and a change from Jack's two previous daughters. So, before his newborn son took his first steps, Jack scheduled. He was going to raise him right—no mistakes for him or his son. He would teach him respect, love, and humility. He would interject when needed and step back if a lesson had to be learned. At six years old, his son would begin school. By eight years, any available talents would be developed. At thirteen, Jack would sit him down and explain the workings of life and what it meant to be a man. For his son's high school experience, Jack planned for good advice being put into action while a guiding force would always be there to put him back on track. College was written in bold on Jack's calendar, and his son would do well for the money it would take. Graduation—job—career—Sunday visits with the grandchildren. It was a well thought out timetable—much like the two before. Jack smiled as his nine-month-old baby looked up at his father's gaze and took his first step. Jack was elated by the motivation apparent in his offspring. He picked him up, kissed him, and gently tossed him in the air to instigate a surprised giggle from the infant. He was beautiful.

Time froze again. The father sat down with his son, gently lulling him to sleep with his steady heartbeat and controlled breathing. Two kids later, and the magic never stopped amazing. As a dad, he always knew that he'd never stop loving his kids. He'd always be there for them—supporting them, loving them, giving his life to them, but still welcoming them to live the lives they had been born into. Nothing could break his love for them. Happiness was such an easy thing to find in his house, the father graciously thought as he laid his son in the crib, and slid down into a seated position against the wall a few feet away. He'd be there when his son woke up.

*17 Jan. 2005*

*I love my dad so much, and all he wants to do is help. His dedication to me is just so passionate—when I hurt, he hurts more for my suffering. I can't talk to him. I love him too much.*

The schedule had been slightly altered. In the slot of what was probably "TBA," a threatening roadblock to life was inserted into Jack's plan for his son. Mike was sick and wasn't getting better. Nonetheless, the plan was kept on schedule. Mike strove to finish high school, and Jack participated with advice and warnings along the way—it's all he could do.

The father was on his knees begging for his son's revival. He cried after almost every time he saw Mike. He hugged his son for the both of them. He wanted to squeeze all the pain out, all the while holding on to what was so dear to him. Mike quietly suffered each day, but always put on a well-lit show of optimism to confuse his audience. However, those in the front row—especially his parents—could always identify the onstage tragedy.

Most of the time, Mike carried on as if nothing was eating away at his body. Each step was a mission, and each smile was a desperate attempt at happiness. This knowledge was only available to Jack through his wife, Kathryn. Even if Mike had the sniffles, he always went to her for motherly comfort, but Jack knew marriage to be a complete, unified team effort. If their son was having problems, he should come to both his parents. Jack tried telling him this—over and over. In his head, Jack would wonder about the qualities Mike might think his male parent was lacking—strength?

"Michael, I am strong." He had stopped the car after picking him up from school.

Wisdom?

"Son, I've been through a lot. You know, my experiences have taught me so much." Jack was now standing in front of the blinking TV.

Courage?

"Remember that time I jumped in that rip tide to save those two kids? Stop chewing for a second. I'm trying to talk to you, Mike." Jack had just bought his son dinner. The worried queries had become an ongoing quiz for his tiring son, but Jack was telling him things that his son already knew. He knew that his father was all of these things.

It was a faltering winter night that seemed to be trying to sneak spring into the city under the cloak of the darkness. Jack's heartbeat ran parallel to the pitter-patter of the melting icicles just outside the window. Kathryn ran her brush through her already tangle-free hair another time too many, and the neighbors were obnoxiously bidding farewell to their party guests out in the street. Mike was rocking an office chair on the floor directly above Jack's room—keenly locating the loose floorboard, making a rhythmic whine of the weakening piece of wood. Jack slammed his eyes shut, waiting for the horror to stop. Kathryn climbed in bed behind him, scratching his back—she knew what torture was at hand for her Jack. Then, the Husband turned to her, grabbed her hand, and held it close to his lips. "I love you."

His wife responded, but his attention was interrupted. *Creeek.* Jack heaved the sheet and comforter off his warming body and shot halfway up the third floor stairs. "Mike!

Go to bed! You need to get on a better schedule!" He groaned his way back to bed—now him behind his wife—and lay there without a word for five minutes.

"How's our son?" He almost felt guilty for asking.

Kathryn, with her back to her teammate, closed her eyes before she could muster an answer. "You know. He's doing all right." She too treated him like a child with a failing belief of Santa Claus.

"No! I don't know!" Jack's voice tapered off into a whispered shout. "No one ever talks to me! My son is wearing away and I can't receive the tiniest bit of emotion from him! I want to be there for him, but I can't! No one will let me! How do you think that makes me feel?"

"Hon, listen. You know how Michael is. He wants to be strong. He wants to *live*, not dwell on his condition." Kathryn tried embracing her husband.

Jack blinked his eyes into the softness of his pillow. "It's just—he never *talks* to me about it. I need him to talk to me…"

Jack's restless sleep kept his wife up all night. The next morning after the husband kissed his wife good-bye, apologizing for Jack's behavior last night, the father crept to the edge of Michael's bed and whispered, "Love you, Bud. Have a good day."

Michael twitched awake—he never knew where he was when first getting up. "Love you, Dad. Watching the game tonight?" Michael had no memory of any sporting event airing tonight.

Michael's dad gave a tired, but genuine smile, nodding. He wouldn't miss it for the world.

Maddie was getting married—his little girl all grown up. Jack unbuttoned his collar. It was sweltering in the banquet hall to compensate for the frigid cold outside. He watched as his daughter put her genetic traits to work. She entertained both sides of the family with her wit, beauty, and intelligence as she gracefully glided across the floor from one table to the next. Jack then turned to the dance floor.

Michael was having such a good time—all six feet, two inches of him towering over his younger cousins and flapping his folded arms like two chicken wings. The father saw the happiness in his son's face and wished it would last forever. The doctors had told him differently last month.

The father of the bride sat alone, contentedly, at a table in the corner of the room. He didn't mind crowds, but putting too much family and too many acquaintances in one room, breathing down his neck, was something Jack could not handle.

*Tink, tink, tink.*

The sound of the forks tapping the delicate glasses resounded throughout the party. The sound was an emotional trigger for Jack, and recalling his own wedding was second nature.

*"I do." Two words that signified the new husband's indomitable devotion to his new wife. He looked into her eyes and saw nothing else but love. He had no plan, no schedule. He didn't want to be anywhere but with her. He knew they would always be happy.*

*Tink, tink. tink, tink.* . The metal might break the glass by now.

"Jack!" His wife hissed a whisper into his ear. "Tell me you have something prepared. Come on, hon. This is important."

He looked into the same eyes he had been lost in for twenty-seven years, still without a plan. It was time for the toast, but Jack had no idea what to say.

"You know you don't have to go." Jack's reflection in the bathroom mirror was looking at Michael with a frightened curiosity, nervously shifting his dotted eyes from his son to the troublesome knot of his tie.

Michael laughed. He knew why his dad was uneasy—his son found a kind of sadistic clarity in his lonesome welcome of death, in contrast to the rest of his family, and most of the world for that matter. "I want to be there, Dad. They liked me." Michael chimed.

Jack hastily undid his tie as if it threatened strangulation. "Okay." He re-thread the black, '70s-style accessory, so thin that it was close to being mistaken for a modern Texas bolo. "Okay. Just—we can leave whenever you want." Jack finished another shoddy knot around his neck and looked to his son again.

Michael slightly raised his eyebrows in recognition of his father's pre-nostalgic gaze, a distant stare from the mirror, looking like there was something missing when it was still right there.

Michael snapped his fingers. "What?" He laughed. "You afraid I'm gonna steal Carl's thunder?" Michael's practiced relaxation with the unavoidable end that was closing in on him helped maintain the attitude he would have hoped for if he were not on the brink of death. It tortured his father, and sadly, Michael knew this.

Jack dropped his hands from his tie, wrinkled from too many recent modifications. His head bowed, his second set of eyes falling from the mirror, and solemnly grunted in a sudden fatigue, "Okay. Let's go, then."

They were both silent in the car on the way there, and after hoisting his son into the wheelchair, Jack waved hello to the best friend of his former neighbor.

"Hey, Ted. How are you?" There was an unparalleled sincerity in Jack's tone, like an infinite source of empathy that could sense, duplicate, and then somehow experience a grief that was never his own. He laid a third hand on top of his and Ted's lengthened handshake as Ted stammered a heavy sigh in reply.

Michael watched in invisible admiration for his father as Jack brought his roaming left hand of sympathy onto Ted's shoulder. "I know. There's never enough time. You're not supposed to be ready." He allowed a moment for silent remembrance that would be mimicked in most of the conservations ahead of them in the funeral home. "He really was something, huh?"

Ted snuffed a laugh past the frog in his throat, smiling. "Talk about living like there's no tomorrow." He shook his head. "You know he tried to convince me to go skydiving with him just last month?"

Michael, still a few rolls behind the intimate bond of the two, maybe three-time acquaintances, shrugged and nodded his head in respect for the dead man.

Both Ted and Jack smiled in thoughtful appreciation of Carl, the man of the hour—best friend, and quiet, respectful neighbor that never left his trashcans on the sidewalk after they had been emptied. "Thanks be to God." Jack thought aloud.

"He's with him now." Ted led the way to the entrance.

Once inside the parlor, Michael proved to be half-right—a viewing was the only place where his diseased frame, highlighted by the wheelchair, could be of some kind of support and relief to the rest of the congregation.

Even the wife, now widow—"You're so brave, Mikey. Carl was always so happy to see you out and about." She was smiling in thankful distraction.

Two or so years ago when this socially voiced pity to his condition was new, this would have made Michael mad, but today–"Gotta keep going for Mr. Reins." He knew what to say, smiling back at the missus' watery eyes.

As Michael patiently rolled past each melancholy, but abruptly uplifted smile to the next, he eventually arrived, unexpectedly, at Carl's coffin.

His nonchalant way about the room steadied as he lifted his torso by his fists grounded on the seat. He cocked his head at the lifeless, sowed up body of his neighbor. Michael wasn't sure what he had expected, but he wondered why he saw the preserved corpse as a letdown. This wasn't Carl—what was the point?

The makeup that covered the skin's pores where the stench of life had seeped out of the body days ago wasn't fooling anyone. The hands were puffed and recreated, and the jaw was clenched in a teeth-grinding manner without the slightest of a muscled, life-like effort. It was the best wax statue of Carl one could expect, Michael guessed.

Michael dropped back onto the seat of the wheelchair, massaging his overused arms and squeezing his closed lips to a tilted pucker. The Carl he remembered from his childhood was a bitter man who was much older than his age and barely left the house for as much as groceries. Everyone else here seemed to reminisce over a personalized, glorified ghost of the man out of necessity, or maybe more simply, funeralized habit.

"Really squeezed in as much life as he could, huh?" Jack put a hand on his son's shoulder, looking at the flesh in the coffin like it was actually Carl. "His buddy over there just told me how last year, this fool—"Again, Jack pointed at the body and laughed with the stuffed Carl as if it was just playing dead to trick the despondent crowd. "—This fool tracked down his ex-fiancé and made amends after thirty-five years!" He paused while Michael nodded in disinterested obligation. Jack relaxed. "She was happily married too, of course. Just shows you, I guess—anything can happen."

Michael nodded again, but this time acutely aware of why he was confirming this conversational information. He struggled for his first words. "It's weird—"

"I know." Jack turned his head from the casket. "It's like he's gonna open his eyes any second now."

Michael was jarred from his deepening thoughts into an unavoidable irony. "What?" Carl could not be further from a wink at this point. "No. I mean—it's like, he did all those things in frantic anticipation."

Jack fidgeted with his tie, nervously honing in on his son's line of thought. "Huh?"

Michael continued, unconcerned with Jack's slowing participation. He wasn't talking to him anyways. "Death, I mean." He paused, unintentionally imposing a dramatic effect on the prolonged silence as he worked out his conclusion. "This closeness to it seems to force this sense of the urgency and brevity of our lives. Like, all of a sudden—anything can be done, and nothing can stop you. Well except—" He glanced up to see his father's horrified look of disbelief, and then quickly dipped his chin back to his chest with a determination to finish. "Well, it stops you." He gestured toward the coffin. "But while you still believe in life, you know?" Michael shrugged. "Must be a great feeling—to die with total faith in the life you're leaving."

Michael took a deep breath. He felt good, sitting next to fake Carl. He then looked up to guiltily catch eyes with his dad.

Jack stood still. His eyes were filled to the lashes with a grief that was all his own, incurable and indomitably commanding the disintegration of hope. He softly squealed behind his veil of tears, barely able to speak. "Why are you saying this?"

Over three years of fighting, and now Michael was really dying. Jack refused to leave his son's hospital room. He held back the thousands of tears that anxiously waited for one wrong move of the eyelid to begin their descent, glossing over his eyes. Not a word was said—there was nothing to say. Everyone had been silently preparing for this moment for more than a year now. Michael had been preparing for about three. Kathryn sat on the other side of the hospital bed, fully alert and perceptive despite not having truly slept for these three years now. Jack couldn't keep a single thought in his head. Every time he reached to capture a fleeting idea of what to say as his last words to his son, his mind would churn and flex until it was empty again. If the nurse outside didn't quiet down, there's no telling what would be left of her in ten minutes

"Mom and Dad, I love you so much." Michael's voice was forceful but short-winded. Jack blacked out as father emerged. "Tell everyone how much I love them. Thanks—for everything." Michael held each one of their hands, and smiling, closed his eyes. The Father faded to the back of the room. Thirty seconds later, he noticed that Michael had regained strength and was talking again, and heard the end of his mumbles—"...going to be okay. Everyone is." Michael's heart stopped beating, and the moment of his death brought a perfect ending to an inspired song. His father would be there, even when his son didn't wake up.

Two hours later, Kathryn and her husband were still in bed. He squeezed his wife's hand. It was time to notify the rest of the family.

*Life is pain. For some, it is not as much the absence of happiness as it is the filter through which all is experienced. Wake, and you feel pain. Smile through it, if you can. Love through it, if you're lucky. Fight. Fall. Cry. Rise. In the end, embrace the pain lest it swallows you. Without knowing, without caring really, you share an anguished way of living with millions before and after you. There is no comfort in this. There is little comfort in anything. Nonetheless, most continue to live through the wonders of a physical body fueled by a spirit that is able to experience ignorance, and knowingly wander into the abyss with a certain destination.*

# part 4

## *michael malone, excerpts*

*January 10, 2004*

*Suicide is irrational, but I died five months ago. Taking more pills in hopes of escaping this pain isn't a suicide attempt. It is a happiness attempt. And what do they treat?—My "clear emotional instability." So f—this journal.*

His body was going into quiet convulsions, and Michael hadn't even opened the transparent, orange tube yet. Tears slowly fell off his hard, jaundiced cheeks—taking their time to say good bye. His eyes were terrified, their usual lush green iced over as they ran as far away as they could from the spotted hints of approaching tragedy. It was a rather large prescription. Michael carefully cupped the manifestation of every failed promise from each of his doctors. His hands trembled, with the weight of death holding the back of his palms to the cold, tile floor. His fingernails tried to peel off his skin in flight of this gruesome scene. An open-mouthed window hurried in a scathing wind, screaming in opposition to Michael, whose hairs pricked and stretched toward the bitter breath of rejection in a final, saddened realization of what was to come.

His lips quivered in total disbelief—dehydrated, colorless, and ripped open with no scab to hide the wounds. His heart raced to complete as many beats as time allowed before its presumed failure followed. Every part of his body thought and acted differently, but Michael could not think, and he could not act. All he felt was the devastating pain that raked with searing hot, sharpened steel throughout his entire body. And it was time for that to stop.

He funneled the white capsules into his mouth, and then swallowed every promise, with pleasure this time. He would cure himself.

Michael never heard his mother's deafening shriek of terror as she dropped to her son's naked, bluing body in her bathroom. He would never remember his mother's promise to him as he was dragged back to health in the ICU.

*"I'm going to fix you, Michael."* Tears dripped Kathryn's message onto her son's unconscious body.

*April 18, 2005*

*Everyone else's perception has become my reality.*

*August 2, 2005*

*I chewed on some fentanyl patches today faster than Fruit Stripe gum. It was okay, I guess.*

*August 27, 2005*

*When someone with less stress or pain or disturbances or aches and pains than me complains—complains about anything—I want to take a box cutter to their stomach, slowly splitting the skin and dragging the ripped flesh in its wake.*

*But I won't even take a fingernail to the thin skin over their ribs; I would despise their screams more than I hate their current foolish existence.*

*October 11, 2005*

*See, you don't get used to pain—ever.*

Michael sat in a warm tub of water, watching the bath oil beads slowly crumbling as the water consumed everything in its depth. Everything about Michael was lifeless, except his eyes. His eyes screamed in horror, anticipating the effort it would take to hoist himself out of the bath and back into the watchful eye of his family. He was completely alone in this world, but always surrounded.

His months in the intense rehabilitation program allowed him to walk again, despite the little relief in pain. Daily physical therapy maintained a somewhat normal level of function, even though it took Michael's full courage and strength to attempt any use of his extremities. Every day seemed worse than the last, as if he had completely forgotten about his condition mid-sleep—sleep that introduced his real-life nightmare to his dreams. Every day was a little closer to death; every step he took added to the distance between him and life.

He reached for the soap like a prisoner desperately clawing between the bars for the keys to the cell, just out of reach, each finger straining for the hopeless desire. His withered body slipped. Without permission, instinct overrode Michael's system and jerked his leg forward to jam the helpless movement of its aching owner. The heel collided with the front side of the bathtub, sending a piercing pain up the leg that traveled all the way to the victim's eyes. Michael could handle the shock—he winced, no more than a professional football player who glances at a scrape on his knee—but his brain knew better than to be exposed to such agony. Michael's will was once again totally irrelevant in his mind and body's opposing direction—shutdown override. His eyes rolled back into his head, curious as to what the brain looked like, and his body went limp in the bath that had been safely drawn to a level of six inches of water. This had happened before.

Five minutes later, Michael woke to a gentle touch of his cheek. His mom was standing, heavily concerned, over his naked body.

"Hey, Bud. Let's get you into bed."

Michael was in no condition to attempt an exit from his watery grave. Nothing had changed.

*October 16, 2005*

*Throwing up has become a regular reaction in my days. I guess it's my best expression of how I feel.*

*I move through my day since that's all I can do—one step at a time, each one feeling like a deathly mistake. I guess it is.*

*November 12, 2005*

*I'm so jealous of everyone that can have a day ruined so easily by a puddle, or a rude stranger, or a bill or… anything. They have chosen their existence and derived some sort of meaning to feel.*

Michael loved basketball. It had always been an escape from the stresses of his life. He could always trust the sound of his backyard hoop's rusted, metal chain that clinked each time he would sink a jump shot. *Clang.* The rhythmic beating of the ball against the rocky, uneven concrete was a hypnotic device to forget the pains and sorrows that were closing in on his back-alley sanctuary. His sisters had both moved, but their problems had not left his parents, and as a young teenager, his own lifestyle wasn't too pleasing to them. *Beat, beat, beat—clang.* It was a sure thing.

A year later, his arena's security walls had been breached. Michael was diagnosed with a degenerative disease—which only meant a prolonged procession to his grave. Doctors had an easier way of saying it. His escape was now just another reminder of his condition. He now focused on every step toward the basket. He would never see an open teammate again—his eyes were undesirably fixed on his legs in order to force and then confirm their function. He couldn't hear the ball making its music with the ground anymore. He didn't want to let go of his protection, but it was hurting more every day. *Beat, beat, clunk*—and then a thud. Michael struggled back onto his feet, after a repetitive dysfunction of his legs, to retrieve the runaway ball that had rebelliously ricocheted off the backboard. Nothing was sure anymore.

*November 21, 2005*

*Today, I watched a baby bird fall from its nest. Its one wing was broken, and its neck was severely off-centered from the rest of its spine. It squirmed with its back on the sidewalk for a while, and then I got a nearby garden spade and tried to end it quickly. My first stab caught the front of its bulging neck while it was letting out a chirp. It squirmed all over. I could hear it breathing as I ground the spade into the pavement, severing the top of its spine, and ending it. I buried the departed a few inches into the soil in my neighbor's garden.*

*December 3, 2005*

*Things stop mattering when you're in pain. I seem to not care as much about the rest of my life. The less I care, the more easily things come to me… everything but relief.*

He didn't feel like going out tonight. It was a Friday, and as his peers carpooled to various parties and get-togethers, Michael locked himself in his room after a week of smiles, high-fives, carefree conversation, and triple tasking (a combination of the latter while still walking through the halls). He retired the persona that everyone else saw. He had finished his therapy for the day. He climbed into bed at eight, and closed his eyes. His face was without expression until he fell asleep.

Asleep, he winced, twitched, and tightened every muscle in his face, horrified. There was no escaping his nightmares. It was just like his time awake. It was the panic of having zero control and the despair of falling through a black hole that had no promise of a final plummet. His life was a dark cave that threatened all unimaginable terrors but offered no tangible fear that could be overcome. Michael was trying to gain energy for the marathon of suffering that he would be obliged to endure the next day. His phone buzzed.

His eyelids shot wide open while his brain transferred the unnerving current of nightmare from dream to wakeful awareness. He wiped the freezing sweat from his face and what seemed to be tears under his eyes. His chest tightened. He hated his lack of fortitude that was highlighted in his sleep. It wasn't fair. He glanced at his phone—six missed calls and four received messages. The calls were his friends wondering where he was. There was a party, and he'd have to be crazy to miss it. He wasn't crazy, but Michael had no problem with missing it. The messages were the other side of his social life. He probably could have predicted them verbatim, in order—Ashley, Kylie, Cara, and Sarah.

"And what is your adorable self doing tonight, cutie?"

His ego appreciated the attention. It was show for a good week's worth of hiding pain and acting carefree (high school girls seemed most attracted to a boy with little ambition and a lot of flirting and jokes). He'd send back a unified apology to all four of them—he was "going to take his mommy out for a date tonight." It ensured a sigh of devout affection. Michael rolled back onto his pillows. His mom probably lay exhausted and wide-awake in the room below his. He felt guilty for even lying about a nonexistent dinner with her.

It would be a while before he fell back into nightmare. He opened his backpack, because it was the only thing in reach from his bed. A ninety-four percent on an essay written on the Declaration of Independence that began with "Four score and twenty years ago"... a ninety-six percent on a trigonometry test, despite his obvious mental absence each class (he could barely define a function). He flipped through his outstanding resume of a fictional high school career. An email from his mom to all his teachers was all the homework, studying, and subsequent credit that he ever needed. He didn't care since the grades held no weight in his already written future, but he'd have rather failed.

He recently accepted that nothing was expected of him, but death. Anonymous donations were made to his bank account, and every gift was just a tear away. Everyone wanted to be his friend just to have an excuse to be able to cry at his funeral. He had everything, and he didn't want any of it. He was completely inexperienced in the common world, but had everything to say otherwise. It was the unopened gift of pain.

*March 12, 2006*

*I watched* George of the Jungle *(1997) the other day. Ursula, played by the lovely Leslie Mann, takes the uncivilized George (Brendan Fraser) back to NYC for medical treatment after her ex-fiancé, Lyle (Thomas Haden Church, who's pretty excellent in* Sideways*), shoots him. Yada, yada, yada—George recovers and brings his antics to the city, and at one point comes out of the shower naked while Ursula has a pretty friend over. The friend sees some things that are off camera, and after Ursula shuffles George out of sight, she exclaims, "Now I can see why they made him king of the jungle." Now, needless to say, this made me pretty angry.*

*Oh, right, George held dominion over all the beasts of the jungle because he had a relatively large penis for a human. They had a measuring contest, and then a unanimous vote on the hairless wonder. Let's not even get into the logistics of other animals' sex organs.*

*... and that's the story of me realizing that I have a small penis.*

*Spoiler alert: Brendan Fraser and Kelsey Grammer aren't brothers like Charlie Sheen and Emilio Estevez.*

*March 16, 2006*

*Meds never help—never seen something like this in modern medicine that can't be at least numbed. I try and stay distracted. Anesthesia was good. Got punched and knocked out cold too—lost some memory. The few times in my life when I was living, but have no memory of it—I win.*

*March 18, 2006*

*Most action in this world is founded by selfishness. A good deed is at first layered with good will and morality, compassion and sympathy, but it is achieved by the need to feed our sense of purpose and recognize the validation for our existence. Instinct serves the individual—to its death if it must—in order to reach fulfillment. The evil in this world is generated by pure selfishness, and so is the good. We are human, therefore we are selfish. Vice versa too, I guess.*

Michael barely lingered on the unnamed vials that he had most likely overpaid for—they were going into his body. Drugs made peoples' lives worse, but Michael knew for certain he had reached the epitome of a ruined life. He shut all family and friends out. A pain that rampaged his body day and night blinded his sight. A high-pitched ring that detached him from all else around him deafened his hearing. He watched his body claw its way from one place to another. Everything was gray. Everything was nothing. He stuck the needle into his throbbing vein.

He refused the name of any of the late-night street products that he purchased. He wanted to avoid addiction—only because it would be too much work to continue the lifestyle of a fiend. Most drugs he only tried once. They all had no effect on his condition's dominating presence. Any current prescription he had access to he took in triple. Nothing. His life wasn't changed in the least. After a couple of months he terminated his illegal, medicinal, after midnight journeys to various corners for a new re-up any dealer spoke of. He didn't have any motivation left. He had spent all of his money too.

Michael lay in his bed, once again locked in his room, asleep and awake in terror. The text messages from hopeful, soon-to-be girlfriends had stopped. No one was excitedly calling for his presence at a party on a Friday night anymore. The Michael they knew had died over the past couple of months despite his regular, ghostlike attendance to school. The world didn't miss him anymore, but Michael did.

*May 4, 2006*

*How come Koalas are so vicious? I want one. I want to carry it around on my back and feed it eucalyptus leaves. We'd fool everyone with our adorable appearance, and then surprise them with our ferocity. I'd teach it how to high-five too.*

*August 7, 2006*

*I don't have much to care about. Even if I did, what is there to really care about–a job? Money? A girlfriend? I wonder how dependent I am on human contact. How long could I go in total isolation? Or, is knowing that people are still out there—living, breathing, sinning, loving—enough?*

Michael sat next to his best friend. He was more than a brother to him. He had stubbornly stood by Michael's side no matter what had happened. They were sitting in Michael's room, throwing a miniature basketball back and forth from relaxed, seated positions. Nothing needed to be said or asked. They knew everything about each other, even if it was never told out loud. His presence was all Michael needed. They were both smiling, really.

By midnight, it was time for their company to end. "I gotta get home, Mike." He said hesitantly.

"You think you could stay over?" Michael knew what his answer would be. He felt guilty for taking so much and rarely giving back to someone that he loved so much.

"You know it, dog!" They slapped five.

A half an hour later, they were both nestled in their sleeping bags on the floor, next to the neatly made bunk beds, ready to fall asleep to Wes Anderson's *Bottle Rocket*—it was tradition.

They slapped five again.

"Thanks for having me over, dude," said Michael's loyal companion.

Michael responded with a smile and, "You the man." Michael was happy.

The next day, the two boys rumbled awake to the music they had pre-set to begin at 11 a.m. They head downstairs to cook breakfast.

"I love bacon … so much." Michael stressed his interest in the meat with a purposefully feminine voice for no apparent reason.

They both thoroughly enjoyed the day together. Golf cart racing (wreaking havoc on their non-membered entrance to the country club's greenery—Michael's favorite), ice cream ("chocolate pleeaasee … with jimmies!"), and girls (Ashley hadn't stopped texting Michael all day) were all scheduled so that each one might be sufficiently experienced. They ended the night together, this time at the other's house. Michael was going to *dream* tonight, just like today.

*October 11, 2006*

*I know I need somebody, but I refuse to let myself find/stay with her. I think it has to be a girl. I think a girlfriend would be good for me—any genuine relationship would be.*

Michael fought for her. She wasn't like the other girls that talked to him. Each one of her rejections didn't matter because he knew that they were going to be together. Even when she had a boyfriend, she'd find notes under her windshield wipers, presents at her doorstep, and roses in her locker. This was no high school infatuation; it was love. He told her everything, not because he wanted her to feel sorry for him, but because he wanted nothing between them—to be as close to her as possible. She playfully resisted his charm, but Michael knew he was close.

On a fall weekend, Michael's parents left to visit their daughter and son-in-law. It was hard to say if Michael remembered his older sister. It was hard to say anything to her to begin with. She stopped saying things a long time ago; she only recited things now, lost in monotony. And it wasn't that Michael didn't understand. There was nothing to say anyways. There never was. There never is. Life came and went, everything in between never effected the outcome. Though he didn't believe this, he convinced himself that he did, and he didn't need to enlighten his sister. He lay in bed as the afternoon quickly dissolved into dusk, waiting for his anticipated visitor.

She came to him. She nervously walked in the house without a greeting or explanation for her arrival. He didn't need one. Michael sat down in front of her. They looked at each other for a long time.

"Want to watch a movie with me?" Michael extended his hand to her, and she pulled him up from the bench. He began his journey to the second floor, and as she followed, she hesitated on the first step. She didn't want to get hurt.

They lay in bed for long past the end of Zach Braff's *Garden State,* both on their backs smiling face-up to the ceiling. Michael didn't want to be cliché, but he needed to recite Zach Braff's scripted eloquence to her: "When I'm with you I feel so safe … like I'm home." He looked to the girl next to him, smiled, and chose silence.

She purposely shivered, and turned her body to rest on his chest. She looked at him, but her eyes made small dashes across her sockets as she peered into his, the way she would have hopelessly searched through a swarming crowd of people for a lost button. Still, she was looking for something bigger. He interrupted her hunt with their first kiss. Their lips met and fit together more perfectly than the last piece of a puzzle. Michael was finally with her. There would be no more talking about his condition and no more expression of his pain—he wanted her to be happy.

Months passed and she was having so much fun with Michael that she nearly forgot about his doomed presence in this world. This was everything that Michael had hoped for her, but he could not ignore the suffering that built on top of his pain. Nonetheless, he continued to refuse her entry into his problems, as he continued to comfort her through her adolescent stresses. He knew it was his fault, and he could not stomach the resentment that grew inside of him. The closer she got, the more distant their relationship became.

It was a Friday night, and Michael had dreaded it all week. He left from the gym to pick her up. As she climbed into the car, it started. She insulted her father's sense of superiority, and disapproved of her mother's over-protection. She gossiped about her friends' meaningless bickering, and she ranted about her teachers' ignorance. She only stopped when she noticed tears dripping off of Michael's nose as he blankly stared through the window in front of him.

"Baby, what's wrong?" She was immediately as close as the parking brake, transmission, and steering wheel would allow.

"Ah, sorry. Just exhausted that's all. You know how I get. I'll be fine." He roughly slid his palms over his face and disbanded any wetness. "Sorry, but I think I'm just gonna head home for some sleep."

"Of course. Yeah, no definitely, Mike." She opened the door. She was ready to run scared back into her mother's over-bearing arms. "Call me if you can't sleep?" She was searching for something to say; she wanted to heal whatever was bothering him right then and there. She really did care about him.

Michael waited to make sure she got back into her house safely, and then solemnly drove off her street. He opened his phone to make a couple of calls.

"Hey girl, what are you doing tonight…? I heard you're all home alone. Need some protection?"

He hung up and sped to his new destination. Another tear fell from his nose, this time landing on his phone's lit screen, still blinking, "Call ended_Cara_1 minute 2 seconds."

He made each turn to Cara's, driving farther and farther from his worried soul mate. He forced himself up Cara's driveway and onto her front porch. He didn't want to hurt the love of his life.

*December 8, 2006*

*I lower my eyes when talking to most people. Not out of humility, but hostility.*

*December 24, 2006*

*"How do you feel? On a scale of 1–10."*

Every day was the worst pain Michael had ever experienced. Ten? He still believed that there were others that had to go through worse, though. So … seven? Was his pain just a sure validation of the true gift of life? Zero? He suffered so much—thirteen?

Michael rarely connected with any of his doctors. They were detached MDs that solved problems for money. At least, that was Michael's only plausible means to treat so much sickness, disease, and despair. They began each appointment with idle conversation and ended each meeting with a handshake and a smile. Did they keep some kind of special miracle drug for themselves?

At this point, he had been diagnosed ages ago, and now spent most of his time visiting various specialists in hopes of a new and groundbreaking treatment. However, he had already lowered his expectations. All an appointment did was guarantee a recited monologue from Michael that academically chronicled his symptoms, which was followed by an uncomfortable and fruitless examination. He provided a learning experience for his doctors. They could marvel at a medical mystery, and then move on with their days.

"Well, Mike, keep working. I know you can do it... I'm gonna prescribe some Ambien to help you sleep." Like Michael wasn't exhausted enough to pass out within seconds.

The doctor closed the door behind him and left Michael and his mom to stare through each other. Who's next on the list?

Michael looked back to the door, where the handle slowly swayed downward, now needing only a small nudge to open and welcome the doctor back in with a wiped brow and exuberant smile.

*Oh, it's Michael Malone? See, I had Michael Fortland's file! He's a goner, sure, but you're a much different story, Michael Malone! You're going to be fine. And Coach K wanted me to give you this scholarship while I was here bringing good news. See you!*

The door never opened, and the handle twisted back into place.

Michael looked down to see his hands clenching the end of his seat. He exhaled past the point of a normal breath, and then denied himself an immediate inhalation.

Outside the door, nurses shouted, bed wheels hissed on the scuffed, tile floor, and heart monitors screeched the deafening song of death.

Michael took a long breath. His mother sat diagonally to him with her eyes closed. In the eye of the storm, it was so quiet.

*January 1, 2007*

*Maybe I don't know what real pain is, but maybe I do.*

It felt like fiery razor blades that hastily hacked and cleaved at the raw flesh that was still healing from a bad burn, shaving off each layer of skin at a time. He imagined his organs and insides to be tossed carelessly around between two baboons—beating them, squashing them, and deciding how to throw them in best interest to achieve the perfect splat on the ground.

It was hard to breathe sometimes. Death would be a blessing, and pain knew the longer it kept him around the longer it could torture him. Every ounce of energy was stolen from him. Every wound was abused. Every muscle felt ripped to shreds, but Michael was forced to take another step. He'd rather bleed to unconsciousness. He wanted to be kicked mercilessly in the head until a coma was sustained. He desired to be damaged until his nerves grew tired of sending warnings to his brain. He felt like Fall's last leaf that if touched, would break into a million shredded bits of nature, but somehow remained intact as the wind ripped it from one atmosphere to the next. He could look into evil's eyes and laugh in its face, blood seeping from between his teeth, for everything had been done before. Burning knives and boiling water to every orifice could not match the pain he knew.

Michael's eyes locked open in the middle of the night. He felt the same as he did every day for the past three years, but as he closed his eyes to drift back into nightmare, he smiled. He felt everything—the thrashing pain and the unbridled suffering—but he also felt the soft pillow under his head, the unmatched warmth and comfort of his house, and his mom's loving touch as she stroked her restless son's hair.

"Go back to sleep, Bud. Everything's okay."

*February 27, 2007*

*I still can't get past myself. What is really stopping me from doing something to help someone else? Am I that selfish? Am I that arrogant?*

Michael sat next to his sleeping mother. He never knew how to tell her how much she did for him. She was giving him some of her own life. They both were. His phone buzzed. He slipped away from his mother, tucked her in, and kissed her goodnight on the forehead. He hugged his groggy father, telling him that he loved him. He tried to help them where they would let him—laundry, dishes, and errands—but he seemed blinded by his condition when he left a dirty house for them to come home to after they had worked all day for the wellbeing of the family. As he exited the house, he grabbed an extra sweatshirt—he knew that the girl he was meeting always refused to believe the actual temperature of the cold outside.

He met her in the usual rendezvous point (an independent coffee shop neatly tucked in a side street of a busy, industrial center), hugging her hello. They were close, despite not talking more than twice a month. They might have even had a chance at romance, but they both knew that too much pain was present between the two of them. She started with reserved, polite conversation, even though they both knew she had called for a specific reason. She eventually faded into her depression. She had been without her mom for three years now, and was now supporting a family of five while still trying to get into the college of her dreams. She was always caught between emotions; she was never sure what to do or where to go. Crying always felt better when Michael was with her.

He never spoke; he only listened. By the store's closing, no spoken resolution had been reached or advice offered, but both left, certain that things would get better. Michael knew he needed these visits, more than she knew.

"Mike," she grabbed him before he got into his car. "Thanks for everything you've done for me." She hurried away before he could give a confused "thanks."

Before he could close his door, another person sought contact. This time it was an aging, homeless man.

"Spare some change, sir? God bless you." He spoke so earnestly, as if he didn't recite this line at least a hundred times a day.

Michael, who usually would see homeless people from a distance and could thus prepare a set amount of money to offer them before he was even asked, was caught unprepared for the urban commonality and pulled out his entire wallet.

He opened it, pausing at the man's obvious realization of the countless bills that filled it, and gave him the lot of it.

"You look cold, man. Here. It doesn't fit me anyways." Michael handed him the extra sweatshirt.

The man was stunned. His reoccurring praise of "God bless you" was the only thing that came from his mouth. For a moment, life didn't seem so hopeless.

Michael pulled out of the parking lot and drove into the night. He knew he should have done more for the wilting, old man, but he was obsessed with getting home in time for his show—it always made him laugh, and at those times, life didn't seem so hopeless. He couldn't miss that.

*July 15, 2007*

*I've written in this everyday this month. Is that a good thing?*

*It changes the world as we see it, causing us to wonder if we ever did experience a life without it. The process of decision-making is changed. Experience and potential become nostalgic folklore, and hope itself regresses to an extremely shortsighted pragmatism. Relief is the only truth by which one begins to live; nothing else seems to matter as you watch your body assume the action of your life. You feel pain, and you are numb to everything else.*

*January 12, 2008*

*I'm totally helpless. People have me, but I have no one.*

*March 14, 2008*

*I'll be gone soon. Someone came and visited. I emptied everything I had in my overcrowded brain into her retreating eyes. She sat for a little and then cried. Strike one. This was the first time that we had spoken since I left her at her house that one night. She wouldn't stop crying, but through the gasps of breath she tried to explain herself. She was like this girl I remember from kindergarten: Her mom gently persuaded her into the line outside of school. The boy in front of her looked sad. She asked what was wrong.*

*He said, "My mommy left me here."*

*"It's okay," she laughed, "she'll be back to get you." She reached back to grab her own mom's hand, who had apparently left her side and—*

*That's how she sounded.*

*She told me that she loved me. Strike two. After some more talking she cried again. She told me she was sorry—she was just going through some things that's all. Of course. I coaxed her through them. We said the final goodbyes that I had hoped to begin the visit with, and then she walked out of the ICU to most likely continue with her scheduled day: "Visit Michael. Check. Cry and have problems solved. Check. Get a DVD for girls' night in."*

*She had struck out, and she didn't even know that I was pitching. She was the girl that I was going to marry. But I didn't want to hurt her when I was gone.*

*March 20, 2008*

*I am so in love with the idea of love that I am so afraid to taint it.*

*March 30, 2008*

*Someone left a note under my pillow that read, "Everything will work out." I cried for forty-five minutes, and wasn't disgusted with myself.*

*April 3, 2008*

*I am a deformed man, but disease will kill me first. I do not know myself. I cannot find him. I do not see the world for what it is, or how it should be. I do not see it at all. I ruin it; I patronize it; I despise it. I need it. I am pain.*

---

*There are some in pain who periodically capture the mindset of those in a supporting role—hope has not completely eluded them. Similarly, there are some around pain that absorb it to the degree that it haunts them every waking moment, torturing their lives as they desperately attempt to alleviate the pain of a loved one. They endure a life that is by all visible means, painless.*

# part 5

## *love*

Kathryn wasn't ready to get out of bed. Part of her had just died. All of the research on her son's disease—forgotten. All of the tears that her sweaters had absorbed over the years had dried. All of her concrete love had become disassociated. If she got up, part of her would never leave the bed, lost in the maze of scattered sheets, pillows, and blankets. Next to her, her husband squeezed her hand. He loved her today—she could tell. It was time to begin to say goodbye to Michael. Nothing was personal anymore—everything, including grieving, was customarily broadcasted to the community nowadays. Kathryn rose from her quicksand of a bed, straightened her blouse, and fixed her frigid hair—mixed with nostalgic, dark blonde curls clinging to energetic youth, and stern, bitter, grey stems that faithfully mimicked her graying soul. Kathryn had missed her biweekly treatment at the salon yesterday.

She turned to her weeping husband who was still seated at his end of the bed. The rest of Kathryn wiped her eyes clear of any moisture and embraced Jack's bobbing head and calmed his quivering shoulders. She put her chapped lips to his forehead and silently mouthed, "We're going to be okay." Jack raised his head enough to meet his wife's eyes, with the story of their lives written in a hazy ring of gold that outlined her pupils and smeared into the smoky-blue centerpieces. Their white backdrops were colored with the tragedy and hardship that each spouse seemed to carry, jaundiced and bloodshot.

She repeated her proclamation, this time out loud. "We're all going to be okay, hon." Her eyes were as certain as the unwavering tone of infallibility in her voice. The rest of the family didn't know about Michael yet. She'd make the calls and let them know, and she'd sit by her phone for the rest of her life practicing her advice, support, and undying devotion to her family.

Emma was an extremely talented, beautiful, and compassionate woman who only needed some direction (that she would never follow). From the first day Kathryn walked her into the first grade classroom (despite Emma's fierce threats that emanated from a linguistically proficient mouth which complemented her forty pound, frail, and ghostly body) of children who were the same age, but twice her daughter's size, She worried. Kathryn wasn't a nail biter, and she nervously refrained from pacing the entire downstairs of the house—that would make her crazy. As a rational and caring mother, she volunteered for every lunchtime duty at the school, accompanied the class to every field trip, and sponsored a class party for every holiday she could find (including Boxing Day, which stumped Kathryn for party favors, so the kids learned the poetry of Muhammad Ali).

*All cross-legged in their assigned seats on the rug—that never could fit the last three kids of the class who arranged a balcony view from the coveted reclining, air-pumped, rotating computer desk chairs—the class harmonized as Kathryn enthusiastically directed her choir: "Float like a butterfly; sting like a bee!!"*

*Pulling her mother aside, Emma angrily expressed with her fourth grade intellect that Boxing Day was not in fact Cassius Clay's birthday but a celebrated holiday when the unsung heroes of the economy were supposed to be appreciated. Not even a celebrated holiday in the U.S.A at that.*

Kathryn watched as her youngest daughter excelled in every academic field entering high school, where her mom conveniently taught French. Besides her three other language courses, Emma opted to learn the language of love by tape. During lunchtime, the French teacher would chaperone the hungry teenagers while the mother kept a watchful eye on her daughter, who sat silently in the midst of the friends she had grown accustomed to after eight years of grade school and now four years of high school. Kathryn's stomach tightened, and the distraught mother made a routine memory check of her child raising. She wasn't a mother that worried about the public eye; she didn't care what people thought of her or her family. She just wanted her daughter to be happy.

Back at home the mother and daughter, teacher and student, sat and talked about their days. Emma had a lot to say.

"It's like she knows how dumb she is, but her stupidity doesn't allow her to realize that talking only makes this more obvious!"

"I know. I know. Still Em, she is your teacher, and ultimately, she means well and doesn't want to be disrespected. You're almost done anyways." Kathryn did her best to reason through the madness. Emma had publicly embarrassed her teacher for the lack of educational substance Ms. Dock brought to her literature course. Following this, Kathryn had talked her co-worker out of a nervous breakdown, as well as neutralizing the threats of suspending Emma. Though, Ms. Dock was a moron.

"Uuuugh." Emma glanced back at her mom. She sighed a smile—she knew she was overreacting, acting crazy, and forcing her mom into awkward liabilities as a teacher who did nothing but work for the benefit of the school, and a mother who would do anything for her daughter. It was okay. Kathryn knew she couldn't control any of it. It was like a gag reflex that was provoked by the rest of the world's disregard for proper behavior (patent, Emma Malone).

"I just need out of this school, Mom." Emma began her tri-weekly trip down the hill. "Everything's just... nothing ever feels right."

Kathryn hid her own uncontrollable emotions of stress and anxiety with a tilt of the head and a similar sigh.

You guide a child through life and cultivate a proper upbringing; you help mold an entire human being, a person capable of doing anything. You have bred pain and suffering, struggle and hardship. There are no more pleasant anecdotes and honest lies that delay the mockery of reality. There is only this hurt—an infection of emotional codependency manifested in parent and offspring that never separates. Some call it love.

Kathryn panicked, feeling the sludge of nightmare lapping at her ankles. She hated herself. She hated the feeling that was inside of her daughter, but she knew that she had little time before it took full control of Emma.

It was not the social problems of a teenager, or the unjust depression of imbalanced hormones. Her daughter had searched for this sadness. Emma saw reason in agony through the countered wisdom of Plato's Socrates, and found solace in Frankl's explanation of debt to existence.

Kathryn looked into the sagging eyes of her daughter and saw an uncontrollable sorrow. Emma's face was gaunt—her white skin becoming grey. It was like a terrible addiction—an impossible hatred that her daughter loved so dearly.

There had been no more than a few seconds after Emma had spoke. Of course, nothing ever feels right. Kathryn would weep for her daughter later.

Presently, she intervened, pushing against the devastation that crawled into Emma. "I know, hon. I—" Tears welled up in the bottoms of her sockets. "I love you. I love you so much. Maybe change will be good next year."

Emma nodded, her jaw clenched.

Kathryn took her daughter by the shoulders, made an obvious look at the clock, even though she knew what time it was. "Hey! Change! You better get moving. You have to be at Lindsay's house in an hour!" Her excitement was a desperate attempt to kick-start her daughter back up the hill.

It was prom night, and after three weeks of Emma screaming herself hoarse with protests followed by manic-depressive, tearful breakdowns about her life, Emma bought a ticket and had a friend arrange a date.

"Come on," Kathryn popped up out of her chair, opposing the four hours of sleep she was getting on the regular. "I'll help you put on your make-up."

Kathryn's heart skipped a beat as if it wanted no affiliation with its harboring body's present action. Emma never wore makeup. She hated it.

"You'd like that wouldn't you—your daughter, Emma, just like every other pop teenager! I'm . . . I'm not going!" That was all it took. Emma raced to her room and locked the door—even though Kathryn wasn't chasing after her. The distraught mother made her way to Emma's doorway a minute later and began her counseling.

"Em, you know that isn't true. I love you so much. I just want you to be happy."

Emma's congested, sniffling yells stampeded through the mahogany door. "Well, it's never going to happen, Mom! So let's just move on!"

Kathryn's pleas and Emma's screams continued through the hour until Jack came home. "Stop yelling at your mother! Jeez Emma . . . just stop it!"

Neither of the women respected his inane force, but it was a good enough excuse for Emma to continue her crying in peace and for Kathryn to formulate a new strategy for the battles that were yet to come.

Kathryn stared at the dress hanging in the hallway outside her daughter's bedroom. She looked down at the three pairs of shoes scattered underneath. She smelled nail polish.

She called her daughter's date to explain the dizzying sickness Emma had suddenly undergone. She then brought a couple glasses of water and juice to her son. He couldn't get over this odd virus.

Kathryn lay in bed that night with her eyes closed, watching Emma sob.

The four months after Emma's high school graduation passed and blended into a blur of occupied nothingness. Michael's depreciation and recent suicide attempt weighed on an already heavy life. Maddie refused professional help. Kathryn kept busy through constant worry. Jack became too sensitive to engage. Emma watched—her feeling swallowed by a new kind of anxiety she had not yet pinpointed.

Freshman Orientation was today. She would excel in school; she would do great things. Kathryn nervously hugged Emma good-bye.

"I love you." The mother looked her daughter directly in the eyes. "Be good." They both knew what she meant.

Emma squeezed back her tears. "Thanks for everything, Mom." It sounded recited. "I love you so much." Her second sentence was an improvised addition to the script. The best line Emma had never written. The only feeling Kathryn felt in her stomach this time was hunger.

Emma woke up to a text from her mom almost every day—an update on her worsening brother, a funny story about her obsessive-compulsive father, or encouraging advice left over from the provoked counseling the night before. They talked on the phone at least twice a week. Emma hated her roommates, was sick of most of her teachers (who never tired of praising their brilliant student, Emma) and despised, rejected, and questioned the growing emptiness inside of her. However, she remained at school, and made not even a weekend visit to home. This didn't stop her from telling Kathryn about all of these miseries. But she missed home. She missed family. She missed love. She didn't know how to articulate *these* things to her mom. Instead, she graduated in three years and came home.

Every day, Kathryn worked on something new that might spark newfound happiness in her daughter, a girl who could do anything, but wanted nothing. She told herself everything was going to be okay. She wanted to shake

Emma. She wanted to scream at her. She wanted to shove the happiness down her mouth like a spoonful of peas.

*The seemingly starved, seven-year-old girl refused the little green pellets until the rest of the family had moved on from dinner and the table was cleared. Later in the night, Emma would secretly sneak an alternate vegetable—she knew better than to neglect a healthy diet.*

Kathryn didn't like peas either. She allowed her daughter's disobedience when she discovered her secretive substitutes, but this time Emma wasn't finding another way to stay healthy. She was getting sadder and more depressed every day.

So Kathryn's motherly habits went on as scheduled. The closer Emma was, the more she worried. She was getting less and less sleep. Emma never seemed happy anymore—at home, at work, everything was the same. Kathryn closed her eyes, and put on a thick layer of cover-up to hide the deepening, dark circles that were beginning to seep down her cheeks. Maddie was in town for the weekend, and she was meeting her for lunch.

Kathryn's firstborn was home for a visit. Maddie was older now. The once sarcastic and unruly daughter now greeted her parents with matured and controlled excitement.

"Hiii, you two! Wow, you guys look great!" She over-exaggerated each exaggeration, and quickly moved into hugs, avoiding the initial eye contact and worried scrutiny of her mother.

Maddie continued to obsessively rub her deteriorating fingernails inwardly against her sweating palms. She had intended to leave her problems outside of her visit, but this was hard to do when these issues were the reason for her hopes in finding security here. Maddie missed the comfort of a familiar place. This was her Neverland—a place that recognized her infinite potential, but never expected her to leave and fulfill it.

Kathryn embraced her daughter with a healing touch—the kind only a mother had, and left Maddie feeling naked and cold when it ceased.

Maddie continued to paint her façade. "Oh my gosh, I love the house, Mom!" She was barely through the doorway. "Is this a new painting?" Her father proudly took command and led her through the hallway like a tenured curator while intelligently recalling the artist's historical background.

Kathryn made her way to the kitchen and hypnotically began washing the dishes. She knew her daughter—the same daughter who cooked for everyone when struggling with an eating disorder, and the girl who showcased her intellect after receiving grades and evaluation below her expectations. Kathryn ripped the dried noodles off of a plate that her husband had ignorantly left in the sink over night. Something was wrong.

By eleven o'clock that night everyone was ready for bed, but nobody was ready to sleep.

"Thanks for dinner, Mom and Dad. It was delicious of course." It was Kathryn's classic dish of breaded chicken, more commonly known in the inner circle as "company" chicken. Why they had it tonight Maddie didn't know, but it was her Mom's—which meant a special ingredient that no one else could taste.

Kathryn chuckled at her daughter's startling enthusiasm. "You know I make it with love, Mads." Her face then quickly shifted to that of a concerned mother.

By silent direction, happily, Jack headed upstairs, his empty criticism acting as a diminuendo to his exit. "Love sure does dry out the meat..."

Maddie shook her head. "He really never quits."

Kathryn responded with a roll of the eyes and a playful threat. "No more home cooking for him." She wasn't serious, but the insults to her cooking did hurt sometimes.

"Not that I pay the bills or anything... laundry is in the washer." Jack laughed obnoxiously until his door was closed, securing his victory.

Kathryn sighed and then shrugged, making it clear that she had chosen him, that she loved him.

Maddie wasn't convinced. "How is he?" as she nodded to the cracked ceiling above her head in a disapproving way.

"Oh no, no we're fine. It's our game. I'll scratch his back tonight. He's like a puppy." Fine or not, Kathryn wasn't worried about her marriage—it was Maddie's that she had honed in on.

"So..." The mother allowed time for any interjection, more specifically a confession from her daughter. Silence—just Maddie furrowing her brow. "How's Bill?"

Maddie knew her mom all too well. She wouldn't dare enter the house without being prepared. "Oh, you know. He said he's sorry for not being able to make it—he's just tired... you know. I left him to have fun with his brother."

If his brother was extra-chocolate ice cream she had left in the freezer, then she was telling the truth. She wanted to tell her mom everything, but the woman was dealing with enough—Emma, Jack, and Michael's condition was wearing on her. Kathryn watched Maddie's eyes retreat, and witnessed her daughter's lips dissolve the budding words that could not escape the throat.

She felt her daughter's hesitation in the short breath before Maddie lied—"Sorry, Mom. I'm a little tired from the trip. Care if I head to bed? Movie tomorrow?"

This was not the type of response that Kathryn wanted. What was she supposed to do with all this advice? "Okay, sounds good. Night, hon." She was now readying for a wrestling match for ample sleeping space with her presumably already asleep husband. She smiled while her eyes unfocused, and blurred the space where her struggling daughter had stood. The bickering was apparent, but she could always count on it. She could always count on *him.* She lay half-asleep most of the night. Though she was immune to Jack's movement, Maddie's stealthy tip-toes across the front bedroom, and the more profound hisses and clicks of phonetic residue within her daughter's shrilly whispered, telephonic arguing caused Kathryn's stomach to wrench inward and tie another knot.

The next day consisted of various ploys by Kathryn to invoke any factual evidence from her daughter. She just wanted to comfort her.

"I'm glad you came up, Mads."

"Me too, Mom."

"But don't you think you should save Bill from his brother." Kathryn was recalling her sole encounter with his brother—the drunken escapades on Maddie's wedding weekend.

Maddie giggled. "He's fine, Mom. Come on, it's too cold out here. Let's get some soup and sit by the fire. Remember how we'd cuddle up under our comforters and have the entire snack cabinet at our feet when Dad would leave?" She hooked arms with her mother, who was grasping for any comment to help relieve her daughter's secret burden, and drove her toward the front steps of the house.

That night, Maddie kept her mother quiet—about real life at least. They went to a cliché romantic comedy, leaving Jack to keep Michael company. They shared a large popcorn, sat front and center to the screen, and laughed at every other moviegoer.

The previews began.

"Ooh. That looks good."

"I love her."

"Eh . . . We'll tell Mike about that one."

"What are we seeing again?" Maddie's bubbling laughter (that she made little attempt to reserve) broke through the introductory song of the featured movie. The two teenagers, who were incorrectly but justifiably characterized by the rest of the crowd in the indiscriminating darkness, discussed it from opening scene to ending credits.

The ride home was dominated by their memorization of every song on the *Sleepless in Seattle* soundtrack—it was their favorite.

Retiring the engine, silence took a deep breath. "I wish Emma had come ... " interrupted Kathryn.

"Me too. But you know how she is. She'll be okay, Mom." Maddie put her arm around her mother, trying to shield the negative flow that entered Kathryn's body.

"Are ... *you* okay?" Kathryn took Maddie's arm off her opposite shoulder and then took both of her hands and put them in hers.

Maddie slouched at least four inches, and began a series of disappointed stutters. "Mom ... It's ... Look ... Why, Mom?" She tore into the house without an answer.

Kathryn followed soon after once a conversational agenda had been predetermined.

Cracking Maddie's door, she began, "How is Bill ... really Mads?"

"Stop it, Mom! Just stop it!"

Kathryn had heard things similar to this before.

"Maddie, you just have to–"

"No, Mom! You can't fix this! You can't fix *us*!" Maddie broke down. "None of us! Not Emma, not Dad, not Michael ... "

"I just want everyone to be happy, Maddie." Kathryn took a step toward her daughter.

"I'm trying Mom! I am! But you have enough to handle!"

Kathryn waived off her abrupt attempt at closure to the conversation. "This is just how it works."

"No, Mom! And it's not fair. It's not. Your happiness can't be dependant on ours! I didn't come this weekend to talk to you about my problems! I came to enjoy my time with you! And I did! I did, Mom!"

Kathryn was stunned. She didn't even notice the tears streaming down her face. She took another step forward. She wanted to *be* hugged.

"Kath–" Her husband swung the door wide open, letting a cold wind hurry into the toasty room. "We need to take Mike in."

Arms now dropped, Maddie hesitated, "Should I . . . "

"No," Jack interjected. "We'll keep you posted. He's doing okay for now."

"Bye, Mom. Bye, Dad. I love you."

Jack had already raced back upstairs to retrieve Mike. Maddie was peering through her misty windows for eyes directly at her mom.

"I love you too, Maddie. I'm so glad you came this weekend. I'll be in touch with you. Say some prayers for your brother. He's been praying for all of us."

---

It had been a month since Mike had been home. The hospital might very well participate in his final moments. Kathryn and Jack knew this. They barely left his side. The rest of the family didn't know this. They came every moment they could.

On a Monday night, Kathryn and her husband sat bedside to their dying son.

"Mom and Dad, I love you so much." Michael's voice was forceful but short-winded. "Tell everyone how much I love them. Thanks—for everything." Michael held each one of their hands, and smiling, closed his eyes. Jack faded to the back of the room, unable to fully accept the reality of the moment.

It took Michael's entire life to witness his mom lose all composure.

"I'm sorry, Michael." She was choking on her sadness. "I'm sorry I couldn't fix you." She burrowed her head into his pillow while gasping for air. Her life was being sucked out of her.

Michael used all of his strength to pull his mother's eyes up to his. "I'm not broken, Mom." He would have cried, but he had no more tears to give. "You saved me. Every day, you saved me." He summoned the remaining energy that was forever leaving him. "No matter what I did or how I felt—you were always there for me. You made me remember why it was so sad that I would be leaving before most. But I'm not sad, Mom. I'm closest to death, and finally *alive.* His mother blinked two tears for every word that he spoke. "You're going to be okay. Everyone is." There was no more energy to prove sincerity, or to believe in his words. He made a statement that he meant to say, and that was all. Michael's final breath.

Kathryn waited for her son's chest to gently lift the sheets one more time, but it was over. Her son was dead. She lived, and he died. No matter what she did, she couldn't change it. When he was alive, she had loved him so much. Now that he was gone, all her love did was make the pain worse.

She stepped back from his bed, and looked to the nightstand beside it. She picked up the same blue journal Michael had scribbled in over the past four years. It was to be mailed to the address written just inside the flap.

Kathryn wanted to delay the errand for as long as possible, to hold on to this duty, asked of her by her son, until the day she died. But she couldn't. She'd deliver it to the house's mailbox herself, and save on postage.

# part 6

## *ends meet*

Jack lay on his back in bed, pools of tears unable to fall from his eye sockets. The funeral was in a couple hours. He rolled onto his side, wiping his eyes on the sheets in the process. His wife—motionless, expressionless—lay beside him.

He spoke to her. "Remember when you brought Mike home from his first day of pre-school?"

Kathryn tilted her head toward Jack.

He continued. "And he was raving about how he could run through walls, and—"

Kathryn strained her voice, even for a whisper. "He said…" Her eyes tightened and her lips twisted. Her forehead crinkled and her jaw clenched. "He said, 'anything is possible if you believe in it.'"

Jack grimaced, watching his wife finish the memory. "I love you so much."

Kathryn broke, cradling herself in a fetal position and crashing her head into her knees with every coughing beat of hysteric grief. "What do I do?" she gargled with a new volume of heartbreak. "What do I do?"

Jack nearly lifted her entire body off the bed, holding her with as much ferocity and as much delicacy the conflicting adjectives would allow.

He whispered, "You keep loving." His eyes closed, his cheeks raised as high as possible to stop the threatening storm of tears, causing the corners of his mouth to curl upwards. He sucked in a breath, and said for a second time, "you keep loving," as Kathryn calmed to a silent whimper into her husband's chest.

An hour later, Jack had checked on the kids, gotten ready, and agreed to meet Kathryn at the Church. He wanted to be there in order to smooth out any last minute arrangements.

Funerals are so anticlimactic.

The girl sat estranged from the rest of the congregation, and fidgeted in the back pew of the church. Faint echoes of the distant ceremony floated like bubbles in the dark, wooden arches above, popping and leaving only a soapy residue to carry on their memory. Truthfully, she hadn't planned on listening to the service anyways, and her distance from the coffin in the front of the church well represented her relationship to the deceased when he was alive. Her only contact with him was an ingenuous letter of encouragement prompted by her mother. In fact, she had envied Michael's illness—it would end. She hated Michael for the same reason she despised everyone else: no one could ever know her pain, and their sympathy was just a curt reminder of her crippling isolation.

Now, he had given her his journal, which she read all the way through last night, save the last entry. He had suffered—she didn't need his personal journal to know that. Her attitude quickly changed when she reached the last note. Her name was written in the margin instead of the date.

Michael's mother approached the pulpit to deliver the eulogy. From where the girl sat, the most audible of sounds over the church's poor speaker system were the mother's staggered breaths and choked words. The girl didn't want to hear any of it.

The cracking of another syllable bellowed across the speakers like a hostage's inarticulate cries through a dirty sock. The father went up to the pulpit and guarded his wife's shoulders from behind.

The girl cringed at the image, and watched for a moment. She looked back down at the journal and read the last entry, addressed to Jessica.

> *I couldn't thank you enough for your kindness, and you amaze me with your sincerity and optimism. So when I say that it makes sense that you are dealing with such a great deal of suffering, it is because those who do always seem to develop such an admirable perspective on life and its true beauty. Don't lose it. Don't forget that*

*this pain is a certain reminder that we are alive. We have life; it does not have us.*

*You mention the effort it takes to even maintain a semi-regulated lifestyle. It oddly comforts me hearing this from you because I have felt so guilty for my lack of relative progress in this world. I've been struggling with this for the past couple years now. I'm not sure where I'm at with it, but I've gotten to the point where I know that I just want my own life—no help and total anonymity as regards to my condition. I'd rather live in shame than in pity. Humorously, my other disease is pride.*

*I am strong, without a doubt, but I have most definitely lost a certain motivation that I first began with as I set off on this path. It's been five years now. My life to others has become so much of a lie that now I have nothing left but to build upon it and hope for an occasional window of support (like the one you have just allowed for me, but sadly it's all I will allow for myself).*

*I tell you this because I believe that you must fully embrace your suffering. Take it in with open arms. Talk about it. Share with your family. Do not hide your feelings, and let the ones you love become a part of your experience. No, there is definitely nothing wrong with wanting to put on a smile to feign everyone around you, but you will never trick yourself. They love you so much and want nothing more than to be there for you every step of the way. These are the amazing lives we have. Enjoy your life with them and everything around it. Make it a real smile on your face.*

*As for me, on top of my pain and suffering, I have added unnecessary stress and caution to any relationship I take part in. My clear desire for any deep relations with my friends and family has been trumped by my selfish fear of "burdening" others with my struggles, when in reality I am only hurting them more by rejecting their love and care. I do not know why I do it. I think I believe if I allow everyone around me to come in, I'll never be able to get out. I have convinced myself that this emotionally stolid and calloused person I have developed is somewhat of an escape from my real life.*

*I am afraid if I lose this well-built facade then the pain will drown me, and yet I sit here writing to you as if I've already given up. I promise you I haven't. I am obliged to fight for every day with my physical therapy and the needed focus to do the things I love. All the same, I do love these things. I do love these people. That is why I am still here—all of this. I am here for this beautiful world of goals, dreams, ambition, selflessness, laughter, and, most importantly, love. I am here for this wonderful world of pain, depression, failure, selfishness, frustration, sadness and exhaustion. My pain and suffering will never take away these things; it narrates, in perfect articulation, of what it truly means to be alive.*

*So maybe everyone is wrong. Maybe we can't change some things, and maybe those things can only change us. But it is so certain that most of it does not matter. We make these events what they are. We love them, hate them, and are tortured and uplifted by them. What's important is how we react and involve these moments in our lives. How we choose to live—in pain, in happiness, with passion and potential, in intimacy and love.*

Jessica hated herself for crying. It took a long time for her to look up from the page. It did not make sense.

The procession had exited out of the side of the church. Only a woman and her husband were left in the front pew.

Jessica closed the journal, stood up, and quickly straightened out her dress. She turned and pushed through the large, rear doors of the church, hurrying to her car. It had been a long time since she had cried into her mother's sleeves, and even longer since her dad's last hug—each Monday, she dropped to her knees, sitting on her heels, asking his tombstone for just one more.

Through her tears, she watched the slithering line of cars turn the corner toward the graveyard.

A whining hinge sounded in the back of the church. Maddie was still sitting in the pew, Bill, her husband, forever next to her. He went for her hand, and she fit her fingers into his. As she cried, he pulled her closer. She whispered from the back of her throat, swallowing the tears that ran down her upper lip in the process. "I'm not sick, Bill. It's–" She choked, and fell into Bill's arms. "I'm pregnant."

Husband exchanged tears with wife, and Maddie lay calm in Bill's shaking body. She listened to his incomprehensible delirium of happiness, muffled by a growing film of tears and mucus. She felt every moment, every heartbeat, and each contact with the love of her life. This was the past, present, and future. She was so safe, as she remembered her wedding day, and how much fun her brother had, just weeks after his diagnosis. She couldn't help recall the most loving things her dad had said to her in his toast.

*"... Seriously though Mads, I love you so much. You and Bill are going to be so happy. You have love—don't forget it."*

She gripped Bill's hand even tighter as they left the church. She won't.

Adjusting to the sunlight, Maddie made out her sister's car across the street. She strode toward it.

Emma sat in her car, and consciously breathed in her oxygen and let go of her carbon. She could breathe again.

As she looked out the window and watched the hearse pass, her eyes gave no entrance to grief, or desperation, or devastation. They gathered the action of the world in a sedated manner: Michael had been sucked dry, sewn up, perfumed, and placed in the box that was inside of that car. Another car passed, and another. Michael was very far away now.

Emma bent her neck, and looked down onto her open palms on her lap. She struck her forehead with the insides of her wrists, and pressed them to her temples as hard as she could. Her upper body wrenched toward the steering wheel, and then shot to the back of her seat. Her feet dug into the car floor, and her legs squirmed, randomly lifting her entire body from the seat. She opened her mouth to scream, but nothing came out but anguish.

Her legs crumpled, leaving her body to fall onto the steering wheel. Her arms lay limp at her sides.

After a few seconds, Emma gulped for air. She sat up.

Her breathing slowed to a calm pace, but she stopped blinking—even her eyes stopped involuntarily following the crawl of the funeral procession.

Entire sheets of tears fell in a redeeming, cleansing fashion down her face. Emma closed her eyes, and smiled.

Two, sharp knocks were made on the passenger side's window. Maddie was hunched in front of it, repeating, "Are you okay? Let me in."

Emma unrolled the window. "I'm okay. How are you? Hi Bill."

Bill smiled weakly just behind Maddie's shoulder.

Maddie sighed. "I'm … let's get to the cemetery. I'd like to be with Mom and Dad."

Emma nodded. "Me too."

Emma pulled the car from its spot in front of the Church and caught the tail end of the procession. On the corner, waiting to cross, stood a young girl, her face dirtied by smeared makeup and black clothes looking oily with wetness. Emma did not recognize her, but still knew who she was. Michael mentioned Jessica a lot this past month.

# part 7

## *an ending*

"Hey, Kath. How are you feeling today–any pain?"

She could barely breathe. Her son was dead, and it was the worst pain she had ever felt. This wasn't what her doctor was asking about.

Kathryn's eyes unfocused and drifted to the wall on her right, where a chart of warnings against the common cold hung. Her voice reflected the vacancy of her stare. "No, actually I don't feel as much today." Her tone was metallic, and a droning vibration formed her words, rather than the expected inflection of a voice.

The doctor was almost too comfortable with dealing with a life-threatening disease. He had been treating

Kathryn for most of her life—and her son for the same condition up to a couple of days ago.

"Good, good. Well, keep doing your therapy and stay with your prescription... See you in a week, Miss Kathryn."

Kathryn rose with little effort, in a fluid elegance, and barely left a dimple of imprint on the thin tissue paper that covered the patient table. She shook her doctor's hand, looked straight through his eyes without knowing whether or not he was looking back, thanked him, and walked out of the hospital—each, floating step with a familiar clip of death at her heels.

There was an emptiness inside her.

Soundtrack to the writing:
Nas' *Illmatic*
Miles Davis' *Kind of Blue*
Common's *One Day It'll All Make Sense*
Eric Clapton's *Unplugged*
Luther Vandross' *Always and Forever–The Classics*
Carla Bruni's *Comme si de rien n'était*